TOTLANDIA

THE TWOSIES - BOOK 5 (FALL)

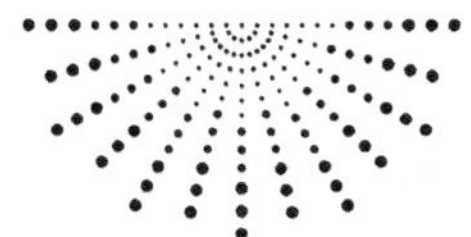

JOSIE BROWN

A BOOK BY

SIGNAL
PRESS

ground for half an hour and you'll realize moms can also be catty, competitive and incredibly judgmental. Josie Brown has that bunch nailed in her new book series *Totlandia*. Picture Desperate Housewives and *Sex and the City*. *Totlandia* would be the babies they'd create. The book is a blast, packed with humorous punches between these ladies whose very existence relies on their ability to keep up appearances. This author will have you howling as you devour this most recent work. Yeah, she's that good. And so are her books.

—*Stress Free, Baby*

"Who knew that joining a mom and tot group would be so strife with maneuvers worthy of a presidential campaign? Membership in The Pacific Heights Moms & Tots Club supposedly can guarantee a bright future for your offspring. Although these women are mostly wealthy, there are a few that are just getting by. As the group opens up to new members, each mother has only one goal: to insure their child will have every advantage that money can and can't buy. I adored this quick read and can't wait to get further into the lives of these women. There are some really sweet moments mixed in with the catty wonderfulness that Brown always seems to capture. I just can't believe I have to wait until the installment which will be released soon."

—*Mary Jacobs, Bookhounds Reviews*

NOVELS IN THE TOTLANDIA SERIES

The Onesies - Book 1 (Fall)

The Onesies - Book 2 (Winter)

The Onesies - Book 3 (Spring)

The Onesies - Book 4 (Summer)

The Twosies - Book 5 (Fall)

The Twosies – Book 6 (Winter)

The Twosies - Book 7 (Spring)

The Twosies - Book 8 (Summer)

CHAPTER ONE

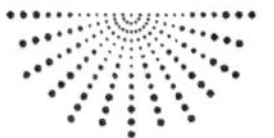

Labor Day
Monday, 2 September
1:01 p.m.

IF LIFE HAD TAUGHT BETTINA CONNAUGHT CROSS ANYTHING, it was to abide by the ancient Chinese military strategist Sun Tzu's most widely quoted dictate:

Keep your friends close, and your enemies closer.

Being Bettina, she took the warning one step further:

Trust no one.

Certainly not those in San Francisco's elite social stratum. When news about her husband Art's financial embezzlement was made public, all reverence afforded the generations-long Connaught name disappeared just as quickly as the city's celebrated tulle fog when hit by the hot, harsh California sun.

The resonance of this philosophy rang even truer in regard to the women she'd handpicked to help her run the Pacific Heights Moms & Tots Club—the organization she'd founded, and had served as its Chief Executive Mom since its inception. Like some of the other club members, at least one or two mothers on the Top Moms Committee had invested with Art.

In truth, there were other ways in which membership had cost PHM&T moms just as dearly, if not more so. Bettina's draconian infractions coerced them into dropping friends who hadn't won the club's approval. They were appointed petty tasks that tested their friendships with fellow members. They were encouraged to report any infractions committed by others who had pledged to abide by the club's endless list of rules.

But now Bettina was the one who was ridiculed, laughed at, and shunned.

Knowing this, she no longer attended the PHM&T's mandatory Monday-Wednesday-Friday meet-ups.

Not that she could, even if she wanted. Her attorneys (in truth, Eleanor's, since her mother held the Connaught purse strings) insisted that Bettina lay low in order to fend off the veritable onslaught of subpoenas from Federal prosecutors hell-bent on unearthing Art's whereabouts. The subpoenas were now delivered almost on a daily basis to her home in the Summit, the Eichler-designed high-rise condominium that was the crown jewel of San

Francisco's Russian Hill neighborhood. To that end, all meals and other necessities were ordered by phone, and received by Benny, the Summit's concierge, whom Bettina paid a princely sum each week to walk them up personally.

Frankly, the siege against her gave her the excuse she needed to shun her family: her mother, Eleanor; her brother, Matt; and his wife, Lorna, whom she despised above everyone else.

She was determined not to see them, and vowed to stay out of the public eye until she devised a scheme that might actually salvage her tarnished reputation.

Today, she put that scheme into action by calling a meeting of the Top Moms Committee. As its Chief Executive Mom, it was solely within her purview to do so. Emails to its members went out exactly twenty-five hours before one o'clock on Labor Day Monday. That way, she held onto the element of surprise.

The ironclad contract they so capriciously signed for the honor of being a "Top Mom" left the women with no other recourse but to attend. Or, as the husband of one of the ladies put it, "This damn contract makes the Iran Nuclear Deal look simple! But reneging on even one of your fiduciary duties as a Top Mom could tie us up in court for years—and that would bankrupt us! Sorry, honey. You'll just have to suck it up and go."

Round One to Bettina.

And so, instead of taking their children to one of San Francisco's many beautiful parks on this crisp blue Labor Day, the Top Moms—Sally Dunder of the soon-to-be Threesies group, Mallory Wickett of the soon-to-be Foursies, and Kimberley Savitch soon-to-be Fivesies—congregated in front of the Summit.

And then, *en masse*, they entered the private elevator that would take them to Bettina's penthouse apartment.

The elevator door finally opened into a seemingly endless hallway crowned with a replica of all twenty-three panels of the Bassae Frieze, the original having been ransacked from a Grecian temple, thus allowing British Museum patrons to gaze upon its intricate beauty.

Joanna Blunt, the Fivesies' former Top Mom, was already waiting in front of the Crosses' massive double-entry doors. She was just as shocked to see the other ladies, as they were to see her.

Sally, the most guileless of the group, and therefore the least likely to keep her feelings in check, blurted out, "What are *you* doing here?"

Mallory's snort did not discern between Sally's bluntness and Joanna's annoyed wince. "You served your time and got a reprieve, Joanna—or have you forgotten?"

Mallory's prison analogy was certainly apt, considering that a sentence for first-degree theft would be shorter than their five-year terms on the Top Moms Committee. The fact that Joanna's daughter, Chloe, was now in first grade at the very elite Pacific Heights Country Day School—ironically, the very same school in which Bettina's daughter, Lily, would soon be attending kindergarten—released her from any further obligation to be at Bettina's beck and call.

Joanna shrugged. "Believe me, I've been asking myself that very same question from the moment I received Bettina's cryptic email"—she glanced down at her Patek Phillipe twenty-four carat white-gold watch—"twenty-three hours and fifty-two minutes ago. The only thing I can come up with is that after having put up with that bitch for the last five years, no way am I going to miss out on watching her grovel and plead for our friendships. Isn't that why you're here too?"

The smile on the other women's faces proved she'd hit her mark.

She scanned the group. "Jade isn't with you? Ha! No surprise there, I guess. My God, if my husband had lost the amount of money Brady invested with Art, I guess I'd have blown off Bettina too."

All eyes shifted to Kimberley. Her face was even redder than her long auburn hair. Like Jade and Brady Pierce, she and her husband, Jerry, had been victims of Art Cross's embezzlement.

"And, besides," Joanna continued, "like the rest of you, I have a morbid curiosity as to what Bettina has been up to in the six weeks since her hubby went on the lam."

"Well, you're about to find out." Bettina's pronouncement roared through the hallway.

The women gasped in unison at the thought that Bettina had heard them.

Even as they shrank in shame, they searched fervently for their nemesis. To that end, Sally's breathy squeak could have been mistaken for a titmouse. The others turned their gaze to where she pointed: at the frieze high above their heads. Looking closely, they saw tiny red lights blinking within the eyes of the plaster of Paris centaurs, which were so viciously trampling the Greek soldiers beneath their hooves.

Apparently, Bettina not only heard; she was watching them.

Suddenly, as if by invisible hands, the doors opened on their own. As strange as that was, the spook house gimmick didn't surprise Bettina's guests. They were quite aware that Bettina reveled in playing God.

Kimberley was the last one over the threshold. Angrily, she pointed a single middle finger at the closest red-eyed satyr before walking through the doors.

She walked through too, but left them open, just a hairline crack.

Call it payback.

"LADIES, FIND YOUR PLACES, THEN FEEL FREE TO SIT DOWN."

Bettina stood at the head of the massive rough-hewn oak dining room table that comfortably accommodated twenty-four guests. Her luxurious blond hair was upswept casually. Her colorful Erdam Orlando color-block lace sheath, a sixty-two hundred-dollar acquisition made only days before Art's disappearance, did not betray her pregnancy with even the slightest bulge.

Doing so would have been a sign of weakness she could ill afford.

Her dog, a deep auburn Tibetan mastiff that she'd proudly named Prince Vsevolod Ivanovich, stood at attention beside her. When Mallory passed him, he growled.

Mallory paused, but she was smart enough to show no fear.

Waterford cut crystal glasses filled with Evian water had been placed in front of the closest two chairs on either side of Bettina. But file folders, in different pastel colors, stood in for place settings.

Each folder was graced with a name scrolled in elegant calligraphy.

"I didn't know you'd invited us for brunch." Warily, Sally picked up the glass in front of her chair.

The others knew what she was thinking: *Is it poisoned?*

"Trust me, I'm not feeding you," Bettina assured her. "After what I have to say, you won't have an appetite anyway."

"Then maybe we should stand instead," Mallory retorted.

"That's fine with me. But if you faint, don't expect me to catch you." She tilted her head, as if truly scrutinizing her frenemy. "You've put on a pound—or three. My God, Mallory! How could you let yourself go like that?"

Mallory started to say something, but then thought better of it. Biting her lower lip, she plopped down into her chair.

Bettina smiled wickedly. Despite being only a size two, Mallory's Achilles's heel had always been her anxiety over her weight. The others dreaded any Top Moms social outing that included a meal because all lavatory runs had to be made before eating. Otherwise, the sound of Mallory purging her salad might send your lunch back up your windpipe as well.

In no time at all, the other women were also settled in their chairs. Soon, they were deeply engrossed in their files. The gasps were expected, as were the sobs. Every now and again, one or another let loose with a "Why...*you bitch!*..." or "Oh, my God! How did you find out about that...?"

These initial exclamations died off before the thought was articulated, for good reason: even if Bettina knew their deepest, darkest secrets, they'd be damned if the others would too.

The research and surveillance of this intel had cost Bettina a pretty penny—practically her whole savings.

Seeing the looks on the women's faces, she realized immediately that it was money well spent.

Sally, for example, would not like it known that her husband was a cross dresser.

As for Joanna, it was the fact that her husband, a newly minted senior partner in his law firm, was also a top-tier customer on the hook-up website, Ashley Madison, that had her tearing up.

Mallory's husband was having an affair with one of her sisters—the one known to be anorexic.

As for Kimberley, her husband was spending a lot of time—and losing a lot of money—on illegal gambling, as if one big win could make up for all the money Art lost them. Their beautiful Presidio Heights Victorian cottage was already in foreclosure.

When the women were finally done, they sat stone-faced, staring straight ahead. After what they'd read, they were too ashamed to look each other in the eye.

Bettina waited until the last file closed before rising and taking each dossier in hand.

No one dared to stop her.

She walked over to the dining room's sideboard. It was placed below a row of beautifully framed watercolors, each signed by the painter: Bettina's four-year-old daughter, Lily. The only thing on the sideboard was a rainbow-hued ceramic sculpture. It was a primitive work —one of Jeff Koons' first, but one could rightly guess it was a horse. One twist of its raised back hoof and the sculpture slid from its base, which held a small vault deep within it.

Bettina punched in the release code. A hum and a click indicated the door was now unlocked. As she placed the files into the safe, she declared, "I cannot think of a more loving way to show my loyalty to you, my sisters in arms, than to permanently hide your indiscretions from prying eyes. Or, as the eighteenth century French philosopher, Luc de Clapiers, so aptly put it, 'Our failings sometimes bind us to one another as closely as could virtue itself.'"

"What the hell does that mean?" Mallory groused.

Bettina sighed. "I guess I shouldn't be all that surprised that you haven't heard of him, Mallory. He died relatively young, and his body of work is rather thin. So let me spell it out for you." Her glare dared Mallory to blink. "*I own you.*" Her eyes sought out Sally's and then Kimberley's. "And you, and you"—she then turned to Joanna—"And you too. So don't you forget it."

Bettina tipped the horse's hoof. It swung back into its original position.

As it clicked into place, shivers went up the spines of the other women.

Once again, they were her pawns.

The only thing that might call this assumption into question was the thunderous pounding of footsteps as a mob of Federal agents came running into the penthouse.

Bettina stood there, rigid as a statue. Her guests,

lacking her resiliency, shrieked as they ducked under the table.

A SWAT team, wearing bulletproof vests over black T-shirts and jeans, swarmed into the room. "United States Marshals, accompanying a United States Attorney with the Department of Justice," one of the men shouted.

The last of the intruders to enter wore a suit and tie. From the cut, Bettina recognized it as Brioni.

Ha, she thought, so that's how our tax dollars are being spent!

The man in the suit made his way to her. He must have been several inches over six feet because he towered over her. "We have a search and seizure court order, plus an arrest warrant for Arthur George Cross." He handed her a set of official looking papers.

Talk about ruining a perfect blackmailing scheme! Bettina's sigh was heavy with annoyance. "I am Bettina Connaught Cross. Mr. Cross is not here, but do feel free to search the premises, if it would make you feel better."

The man's brow lifted derisively. "So honored to have your 'permission' to do so."

"And you are?" she asked archly.

"Daniel Warwick. I'm the court-appointed trustee for all of Mr. Cross's assets." He looked her over, as if sizing her up. "And yours too."

"I beg your pardon?" Bettina's voice was low and ominous.

Upset by his mistress's tone, Prince Vsevolod mimicked her with his own deep growl.

Daniel stared down at him.

It was no contest. Prince Vsevolod surrendered with a wag of his tail while nuzzling on Daniel's pant leg.

He might as well be kissing his ass, Bettina thought. *For that matter, maybe I should, too.*

With focused effort, she positioned her lips into a smile and leaned in. "I think you have it all wrong. I took no part in my soon-to-be ex-husband's business."

Daniel shrugged. "That may be the case, but the court has ordered the confiscation of any and all property, cash, and assets acquired during the period of embezzlement."

A collective gasp rose from under the table.

Bemused by Bettina's Greek chorus, Daniel crouched down beside it. "Ladies, if you wish, you are free to go."

Bettina's Top Moms didn't need a second invitation. Without a backward glance, they scurried out of the room.

Bettina had never seen the women move that fast, and in heels no less. Except for Kimberley, who gave Bettina's tormentor a wink.

The nerve of that tart!

Bettina's warning, meant for all of them, but now especially for Kimberley, followed them out the front door: "Ladies, I'll see you tomorrow, nine o'clock sharp, in the Golden Gate Valley Library's assembly room. We have some new moms to vote on—not to mention some new policies. Come prepared with your list of favorite candidates."

When she didn't hear their acknowledgments, she added, "And, remember: *United we stand, divided we fall!*"

She turned back around to find Daniel staring at her. "What is that supposed to mean?" he asked.

"They're part of my moms and tots group. It's a personal reminder."

"Yeah, I sort of got that."

Seeing his consternation, she added, "Nothing to worry about, believe me. It's…confidential—in regard to *them*, not me." No better time to change the subject than now. "You and your crew really must leave now." She raised her hands, as if, presto-change-o, he'd simply disappear.

"Mrs. Cross—"

"It's Mrs. *Connaught* Cross. But, please, call me Bettina." She batted her eyelashes, all the while wondering if that really worked in softening the male perspective.

Alas, no. All it gained her was another bemused smirk from him. "Mrs. *Connaught Cross*, once again let me remind you that any property or possessions acquired during the time of embezzlement is subject to search and seizure."

"*Mr. Warwick,* you're missing my point entirely! Art had nothing! You see, everything in this home belongs to me, including the condo. It's all in my name."

"*Bettina*, tell me: was it purchased within the past five years?"

Finally, he's softening up, she thought. "Why, yes, in fact—with money from *my trust.*"

"Oh, yes, *your* trust!" It was almost as if a little light went off in his head. "By the way, any co-mingling of your funds, and Art's, leaves it open to our forensic investigators, and possible seizure as well."

"Ha! Do you think I'd ever let Art get anywhere near my money? I know better!" As soon as the words were out of her mouth, she could have kicked herself.

Especially seeing this Warwick fellow roll his eyes. "And they say, 'the wife is always the last to know'? Thank you, Bettina, for laying that old chestnut to rest. And under Federal law, anyone who knew about his illegal activities and failed to report it is just as culpable."

"I didn't say I knew he embezzled," she huffed. "I meant that I knew he was a lousy fund manager."

"You're parsing your words now."

"My attorneys will beg to differ," she bristled.

"No doubt." Daniel shrugged. "However, this subpoena and search warrant supersedes their personal opinions. But hey, don't take my word for it! Feel free to give them a call."

Bettina snatched her phone off the table. She'd just hit her attorney's number when one of the marshals shouted down from the second story landing, "Yo, Warwick, you've got to get up here to see what we've found in the master bedroom!"

Daniel whipped around. "Is it Cross's stash?"

"Almost as good! It's a bondage chamber with all sorts of dirty little goodies. The guy was one sick puppy."

Oh…hell. Bettina turned beet red.

Her change in color was not lost on Daniel. Smothering his smile, he pointed toward the second story. "I think it's time you gave me a tour of your boudoir."

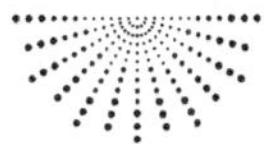

CHAPTER TWO

Labor Day
Monday, 2 September
Also 1:01 p.m.

"I thought you were saving *Hamlet* for next semester." Jade Pierce plucked the Shakespeare play from one of the many boxes beside her side of the bed.

Her declaration elicited a groan from Reggie Pudberry. "If talking about my class syllabus is your idea of dirty talk, we might as well get out of bed."

She laughed as she rolled over toward him. She still had the book in her hand. "We should get up anyway. Besides the fact that I'm famished, you haven't finished packing all the books you'll need for the classes you'll be teaching, and school starts in three days!" She flipped the pages until she found Act Two, Scene 1. "But yes, since you brought it up, it would have been much sexier if you had shouted, *'This is the very ecstasy of love'* when we climaxed."

As she stretched, the sheet rolled off her breasts.

Reggie took this as a signal to yank it off the rest of her body.

"We can't spend the whole day in bed," she pouted. The longing in her voice dared him to prove her wrong.

"*'The lady doth protest too much, me thinks.'*" He grinned. "Sure we can. Oliver is at Brady's, and besides, half the day is already gone, so why not?" He pulled her closer for a kiss.

The only reason Jade came up for air was because her cell phone was ringing.

Like all mothers, her first thought went to her child, two-year-old Oliver. Needless to say, she was relieved to see the call was from her friend, Jillian Frederick. But a second later, relief gave way to guilt. "Oh, hell!" She leaned over Reggie in order to glance at the clock on his bedside table. "It's already one? I was supposed to meet Ally and Jillian at Jillian's house ten minutes ago!"

She leaped out of the bed as if it were on fire.

He looked up from his task at hand—admiring her still erect nipples—and groaned. "What? ...No! Tell them that you're running a little late—just ten more minutes," he pleaded. "I'll make it worth your while."

"So I see, by your, er, tent pole." She nodded toward

the sheet, although still wrapped below his waist, it rose to an impressive height.

She sighed longingly. "I'm sorry, Reggie, but I promised Eleanor I'd do what I could to support Bettina in keeping the club on an even keel through this crisis over Art's shenanigans. She's been off the grid for the past six weeks! But, yesterday I received an email from her. She wrote that there was some club business to be taken care of, and it couldn't wait."

She winced as he groaned. Even more disappointing was the effect of her statement on his tent pole.

"I'm shocked the club is still in existence, what with the number of families who were affected by Art's embezzlement," he grumbled.

"You and me both!" Jade shook her head in wonder. "I don't know if members are hanging in out of curiosity, or if they're waiting for her to re-emerge, so that they can publicly stone her."

"I'd happily buy a ticket to that," he muttered.

"In fact, the club is more popular than ever! For every mother who has resigned from the club, another six have submitted applications. And the applications for the new Onesies is almost double what it was last year." Jade shook her head. "But the Top Moms refuse to move forward without Bettina's say so."

"Little scared mice." Reggie rolled his eyes.

Jade nodded. "Right? And for the life of me, I don't

know why. With all the dirt that's come out on Art, she certainly shouldn't have any hold over them now."

"Or you, for that matter," he pointed out. "I'm glad that Brady was able to roll with the financial punch that Art dealt him."

"Me too." Jade's declaration was heartfelt.

It hadn't always been that way. A year ago, she'd written off any chance of ever seeing her ex-husband, Brady Pierce—or for that matter, her toddler son, Oliver. The former pole-dancer's banishment was the result of having left Oliver, sick and with a fever, in the care of her so-called talent agent while she went for an audition.

When the infant ended up in the hospital, Brady, angry and disgusted, offered Jade a very large alimony on the condition that she stay out of both their lives. Ashamed of her actions, she took the offer. To validate her actions, she did the movie anyway. It was pitched to her as an "artistic indie" film—

But she didn't learn until she was already on the movie set that it was a porn flick.

When Brady called her out of the blue with a proposition that she come back to San Francisco, she presumed he missed her, and that she was finally forgiven. She wasn't. Instead, he had a proposition for her: He'd pay her triple her alimony. In return, she had to pretend they were still married in order to get Oliver accepted into the Pacific Heights Moms & Tots Club. Jade agreed—not because he offered her half a million dollars to take

Oliver to moms-and-tots only meet-ups three times a week, but because she hoped being close to them would remind Brady of all the reasons he loved her in the first place.

Instead, he fell in love with one of her closest friends in the club: Ally Thornton. Despite Ally's vow to keep Brady at bay, the knowledge that he saw in Ally all the things he'd never found in Jade drove his ex-wife to do shameful things—which included divulging two secrets to Bettina that would get her rival kicked out of PHM&T: strike one was Ally's single status. Strikes two and three were that she was a working mother with her own business.

If the past twelve months had taught Jade anything, it was Brady may have always lusted for her, but he had never truly loved her. Worse yet, it taught her that no one would ever love her if she first didn't love herself.

Reggie helped her come to these conclusions. But the way he saw it, she'd helped him first. She'd gotten him out of the gutter and off the sauce, and given him an opportunity to regain his self-respect.

She hated herself for betraying Ally.

Redemption came by convincing Ally to accept Brady's love.

As a couple, Brady and Jade had been a disaster. As friends, they'd found the respect and appreciation they'd sought from each other.

"We've figured out how to get in to see Bettina," Jade

explained. "Apparently, the concierge in her building is gaga over Jillian's pies."

"Why go at all? You're already late," Reggie reasoned. Suddenly, his grimace gave way to a naughty grin. "And besides, you can't leave the house without something in your belly. Did you forget I that was going to make my world-famous French toast?"

That stopped her in her tracks. She groaned. "Stop it! I'm *so hungry.*"

"And I'm *so horny.* He peeked under the sheet and sighed. "Tell you what: you make me happy, and I'll reciprocate. The way I'm revved up, sex will set you back seven minutes, tops. French Toast is another ten, which is time for you to shed any afterglow and leap into your jeans."

He had a point. A very tall one, given the growing height of the sheet.

He got his answer when she climbed back in bed.

This time, it was her turn to pull the sheet from him.

Also at 1:01 p.m.

"—AND SALES HAVE TRIPLED. DURING THE SAME PERIOD OF time you reduced your expenses by eight percent per unit sold." Brady Pierce talked with his mouth full. No matter, what he said was worth hearing him mumble through a piece of apple pie, "That, in turn, led to an increase in your profit margin by another fourteen percent per pie, which means you're clearing above your initial goal of fifty percent net profit per unit sold. So, despite your protestations, Jillian, I say we go for venture capital funding now—and the sooner, the better. We have a very short window." He pointed his fork at the amaretto pecan pie just out of reach. "Hey, Ally, doll face, can you slide that one over too? You know it's my favorite."

Instead, Ally Thornton moved the pie further away. "No. I will not! In the first place, you're talking with your mouth full, which is setting a bad example for the children." She pointed to Jillian Frederick's twin toddler girls, Addison and Amelia, who were torturing their Gund Dollies, with the help of Brady's son, Oliver, and her own daughter Zoe. "Secondly, we don't need you eating up the profits—something you've been doing all morning. And thirdly, this pie is already promised to Benny, the concierge in Bettina's building. It's his favorite."

"Really? You think you can buy your way into her fortress with a *pie*? You're quite a pair." Brady laughed so hard that he almost choked. The fact that his mouth was still full may have had something to do with that.

"Of course we do! It's *amaretto pecan*." Ally's scowl begged the question: *Do you presume otherwise?*

"Speaking of Benny, Jade should have been here by now," Jillian declared. She picked up her cell phone and punched in Jade's number. After several rings, it rolled over to voice mail. "Hey, Jade, are you on your way? Hope so! See you soon." She rang off, and then turned to Brady. "Okay, okay, I see your point—everything with Life of Pie is moving in the right direction. But you forgot one very important thing." She glanced over at her business partner, Ally. "Whereas the shop is finally in the black, covering all of its overhead, and I'm finally making my mortgage payment, it'll be some time before Ally sees a return on her initial investment."

"All the more reason for us to approach the V.C.s. That way, we're playing with other people's money."

"Gee…I don't know. It just seems too *soon*. I mean, we're about to launch our new line of special event pie-lets, and—"

Brady gulped hard before asking, "What the hell is that?"

"A mini–pie, sort of a one-person dessert," Ally explained. "It'll be great for special events, like weddings, so that guests have their choice of flavors. I designed a cute stand that holds twenty at a time."

"In fact, we're debuting the Life of Pie-lets this Saturday," Jillian interjected. "The biggest bridal fair in the San Francisco Bay Area is taking place right down the block, in the main pavilion at Fort Mason."

"Jillian and I are working the show together," Ally warned Brady. "But Barry and Christian can take Zoe any time after two o'clock."

He rolled his eyes. "In other words, they get to sleep in."

"You wouldn't be sleeping in anyway, considering how early this little bruiser rises." Jillian bent down in order to tussle Oliver's head of soft yellow curls.

Brady pulled Ally into his lap. "Since you're going to be there anyway, why not batten down the hatch on our own nuptial shindig?"

Jillian's eyes lit up. "What? Do you mean you two have finally set the date?"

Ally shook her head. "Not quite. We still have a lot of loose ends to pull together. There's the capitalization of Life of Pie, not to mention I have to decide what to do with the townhouse—"

"And then there's a little thing she wants drawn up, called a prenup," Brady snickered. "I've already told her that what's mine is hers, but she won't hear of it."

Jillian clicked her tongue in mock shock. "Ah, the anguishing issues faced by power couples! I'll take the mundane struggle of who controls the remote when Masterpiece Theater runs during football season over who controls the Thornton-Pierce tech dynasty anytime!"

Brady frowned. "You've got it wrong. It's the *Pierce-Thornton* Dynasty."

After recovering from her apoplectic gasp, Ally yanked the apple pie away from him too, setting it down hard on the counter. She winked at Jillian. "I blame it on you. I told him that as soon you and Caleb tie the knot, I might actually give in to his insistent pleas for my hand in matrimony."

"Well, then, I wouldn't hold your breath," Jillian muttered. "As strangely as Caleb has been acting lately, he might be bolting as opposed to putting a ring on it." She held up her left hand as proof that all fingers on it were naked.

"He'll change his mind, the moment you're rolling in the right kind of dough—and I don't mean the kind you use to bake your pies," Brady promised her.

"No he won't, Brady Pierce, because he's not as financially motivated as you. He's all mountain man, and that's the way I like it." Jillian plopped back down in her chair, her eyes closed. When she opened them again, she turned to face her business partner. "Ally, be honest with me. Is it too early for us to be thinking of expanding?"

Ally shrugged. "It's hard to say. I was surprised how fast we've grown in just a few months. Then again, when you have a good product, people talk. And thanks to you, Jillian, our pies are flying out the door."

"Take some credit. People heard about the shop because of your great social media skills and public relations efforts," Jillian countered.

"That's exactly my point! You're a great team!" Brady insisted.

"Let me finish." Ally laid her hand on top of his. "Jillian, the fastest way for us to grow Life of Pie—and more importantly, the quickest way to get you a real salary, and to do so before you burn yourself out, what with all the long hours you work—is to acquire the expansion funds that buys us the time and the manpower to increase our efficiency levels. For that, we need venture capital."

Jillian nodded slowly, but she still wasn't smiling.

Ally reached out with her other hand—this time, to Jillian. "Honey, what is really your concern?"

At first, Jillian said nothing. Finally: "That they won't like my pies."

"What...are you crazy?" Brady slapped his forehead with his palm. "After eating your masterpieces, we won't be able to beat the money men away with a stick—"

Ally cut a wedge of apple pie and shoved it into his mouth to shut him up. "Jillian, honey, what Brady is trying to say is that you deserve the success you've worked so hard to build over these past months. He believes in you, and heaven knows I believe in you. Neither of us would be pushing you to do something we don't feel is a slam-dunk. So please, *do yourself a favor and believe in yourself.*"

Jillian sat silently for what seemed to be a lifetime. Finally, she whispered, "Maybe having a little more cash flow would allow me some balance in my life—so that I can have more time for the girls, and for Caleb." Wearily, she closed her eyes. "Okay, set up the meeting."

"*Yes!*" Hearing Brady's shout, all the toddlers froze at once. Then Oliver started to whimper. In sympathy, the girls did too.

"Oh, my God! See what you started?" Ally sighed as she scooped up Oliver and Zoe and kissed their cheeks.

Jillian did the same to Amelia and Addison.

Brady did them one better: he pulled another apple pie off the counter, grabbed four teaspoons, and slapped them down on Jillian's coffee table in front of the children. "Go at it, kids!"

The children didn't need a second invitation.

As they dug in with gusto, Ally poked him in the side, but then put her arms around his waist. "Your parenting skills leave a lot to be desired."

"You remind me of that on a daily basis." He tilted his face toward hers in order to kiss her lips.

The insistent honking of Jade's car horn gave Jillian an excuse to nudge them away. "We better move it."

"Wait…when does the Cavalry—I mean Caleb —get here?"

Jillian blushed at the mention of her boyfriend, Caleb Martin. "Beats me. He went out early this morning without saying where he was headed, and I haven't heard from him since. He's been moody and mysterious lately. Not that I can blame him. He's taken on a woman with twin toddlers and a new business that has her working practically around the clock." Her smiled faded. "Tell me the truth: should I be worried?"

Brady shook his head. "Nah. He's just the strong, silent type. It's part of the park ranger creed."

Ally snorted. "Oh, yeah? And what is the tech entrepreneur creed?"

Brady pulled her in for another kiss. "Don't get involved with any woman who can't save you from your own ego."

Ally tweaked his nose. "You have all the right answers."

"It's why I make the big bucks." He shifted his gaze to Jillian. "And so will you, now that you've agreed to let me put out feelers."

Jade honked again, just as Zoe let loose with a wail. Oliver was sticking her doll's face into the pie.

While Brady ran over to break up the fight, Jillian and Ally slipped out the front door.

"By the way," Jillian warned Ally, "Jade is determined to twist your arm about reapplying to the club, so be prepared."

Ally snorted. "She can twist all she wants, but it's not going to change my mind. I've already done my penance at PHM&T. And besides, I've got something much bigger on my plate: turning Life of Pie into a household name."

Jillian shrugged. "Whatever. But, considering we all promised Eleanor to create a kinder, gentler Bettina, you'll have to figure out a way to say no to Lorna too."

Ally chuckled, "Yeah, okay, I've been duly warned."

CHAPTER THREE

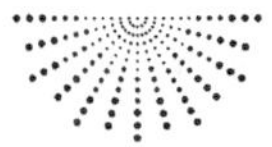

1:32 p.m.

"Lorna, darling, is Matthew anywhere about?" Eleanor Morrow Connaught's question sounded deceptively calm.

Integral to the role of daughter-in-law is the quick analysis of even the slightest nuanced tone from the woman who birthed her husband, no matter the amount of static on any cell phone call between them.

Lorna Connaught was no exception. She waited until her five-year-old niece, Lily, pirouetted onto the terrace to the *Happy* song and was safely out of range before replying, "Sorry, Eleanor. He went out with Dante about a half-hour ago. I don't expect them home for at least an hour, perhaps two."

Lorna hoped that her own tone didn't reflect her

annoyance. Matt's disappearances with their now two-year-old toddler were becoming a regular habit. He'd use the excuse that he was going out jogging, and take Dante in a heavy-duty stroller that stood up to the hills of San Francisco, but he never came home sweaty. And he certainly wasn't losing the slight tire that had settled around his waistline some time after he turned thirty-three.

Not that she'd ever reveal this to Eleanor. She kept her mother-in-law strictly on a need-to-know basis. In Lorna's opinion, Matthew leaned too heavily on Eleanor as is.

To repay Eleanor's many financial and emotional favors, Lorna consented to sharing the CEO duties of the Pacific Heights Moms & Tots Club with her sister-in-law, Bettina Connaught Cross. Lorna's baby was due just a few weeks earlier than Bettina's—another reason she accepted Eleanor's plea to help her daughter run the club that was Bettina's proudest accomplishment.

With Art leaving her high and dry, Lorna did what any Connaught would do: came to Bettina's aid.

Co-president of PHM&T was not a role Lorna relished. In the first place, Bettina had never accepted her as part of the family. Every remark Bettina made either to or about her brother's wife was either downright rude, or dripping with sarcasm.

Not to mention that last year, when Lorna applied to the club with Dante, Bettina made it quite clear to her that no favoritism would be received. That was fine with

Lorna. She looked forward to earning her way into the club, along with the other new Onesie moms—Jade Pierce, Ally Thornton, and Jillian Frederick—now her dearest friends.

With hard work and a little luck, she leapt each hurdle Bettina placed in her path to membership. Still, aware of Bettina's feelings toward her, she felt it wise to withhold the reality of Dante's condition from her sister-in-law. She resisted the urge to tell Matt and Eleanor too. Her mother-in-law had never felt Lorna was Matt's social equal, whereas Matt, who had never known hardship, folded when life got tough.

Had either of them expressed pity or disdain for Dante, she would have taken the little boy out of their lives forever. Instead, they rallied to his aid.

And now that Lorna was pregnant again, she'd never felt more loved.

Or more like a Connaught. All the more reason for her to ask, "Eleanor, I'm here for you. What needs to be done?"

"It's Bettina! Apparently the U.S. Marshall service walked into her place with a subpoena." For the first time since Lorna had known her, Eleanor sounded bereft. "They claim that everything in her home is subject to seizure. It's a holiday, so I can't get in touch with our attorneys. On top of that, Hera talked me into spending the weekend in Bolinas, so it'll take me at least ninety minutes to get back to the city to help her through this."

No two women were more different than Eleanor Morrow Connaught and Hera Harmony, who also happened to be Lorna's mother. Upon first sight, they had circled each other cautiously, like two panthers after the same prey: in their case, the grandson they shared, Dante. In time, their love of music and art—and the *joie de vivre* ingrained in both women—drew them together.

So did the knowledge of Dante's medical condition. Lorna had no doubt that, between his parents and his grandmothers, Dante would never lack the unconditional love that all children deserve.

Lorna knew Bettina would never appreciate her help. Still, since her one and only objective was to put Eleanor at ease, she replied, "She's only two blocks away. I'll go right over to Bettina's, if you'd like."

"Oh, my God—that would be a blessing! Tell her I'll get there as soon as I possibly can. And, in the meantime, I'll keep trying the attorneys. And Lorna, thank you…for *everything*."

Eleanor's genuine appreciation made it all worthwhile.

Lorna tapped the French door to the terrace. "Lily, come on, honey."

The little girl ran in, breathless. "Where are we going?"

"To your house. Don't forget to grab your sweater." Lorna plucked her purse off the foyer credenza, and rummaged through the front pocket for her house keys.

Lily wrinkled her nose. "Aw, Aunt Lorna! Can't we

wait until all those mean Top Moms leave? Please? Pretty please?"

Lorna looked up at her. "Your mother has company?"

Lily's eyes opened wide. She slapped her hand to her mouth. "Oh no! I wasn't supposed to tell you. Please, don't tell Mummy!"

"Of course not," Lorna assured her. She then turned toward the mirror and pretended to smooth her hair. In truth, she was trying to hide her frown. Bettina had promised Eleanor to include Lorna in all the Top Mom committee meetings. Apparently, she'd already broken her promise to her mother.

A raid from Federal agents would give the Top Moms more gossip to spread about Bettina and the rest of the Connaughts.

I have half a mind to let Bettina stew in her own mess, Lorna thought.

But no, she too had made a promise to Eleanor—and she was going to keep it.

Come hell or high water, Bettina was going to uphold her part of the bargain too...for Lily's sake, if no one else's. Lorna would see to that.

1:44 p.m.

Jillian was right. All it took was her amaretto pecan

pie to get Bennie the Concierge to look the other way so that she and her pals could take one up to "their poor, lonely friend, Mrs. Connaught Cross."

Little did she know that, by the time they'd arrived, Bennie had resigned himself to the fact that traffic in and out of Bettina's condo was going to rival that of Grand Central Station, and there was nothing he could do about it.

So, he happily and thankfully took the pie, waving them toward the elevators even as the first forkful entered his mouth.

When the elevator doors opened, the women were faced with the very last people they expected to see: Mallory, Sally, Kimberley, and Joanna.

After the collective shock and chagrin, Mallory chortled, "Ha! I guess the second shift has arrived! Watch out, ladies. Whatever she has on you will turn your hair white."

"Run for your lives!" Sally hissed.

Ally, Jade, and Jillian exchanged bemused glances. *What the hell were they talking about?*

Kimberley was the last one to walk out of the elevator. Her glare, directed at Ally, was meant to make the latter uncomfortable.

To her surprise, Ally met it head-on. She was quite aware that the cold front emanating from Kimberley was the result of the former's jealousy: Before Ally joined

PHM&T, Brady and Kimberley had been lovers. It was his way to ensure Oliver's entry into the club.

The fact that Ally and Brady were now a couple—and not just any couple, but San Francisco's *It Couple*, with all of their high-tech successes—angered Kimberley to no end.

The staring contest was interrupted when Jade bumped into Kimberley on the way into the elevator.

"Ouch!" Kimberley yelped. Instinctively, her gaze moved to Jade's eyes.

The hatred she saw there caused her to recoil.

Suddenly, it hit her: *Jade knows about Brady and me.*

But how could that be?

That bastard, Brady must have told her.

Why else would Jade have avoided her calls these past few weeks?

Presuming that it was the best way to keep Brady in line, Kimberley had worked hard to establish a friendship with Jade. Unsure as to where she really stood with Bettina and her posse, Jade had welcomed Kimberley's fawning attentions. But in the last few weeks, Jade had quit returning her phone calls.

At first, Kimberley hadn't noticed because she'd somehow lost her iPhone. A few days later, though, when she finally gave up any hope that it would surface, she went to her cell phone carrier, who replaced it. Scrolling through the archive of her missed cell calls, she confirmed that Jade had indeed quit calling.

Now that Brady was officially with Ally, currying favor with Jade no longer mattered.

Rumor now had it that Jade rebounded into the arms of that not-so-hard-on-the-eye Nobel Prize-winning professor of literature she'd wrangled for the Fivesies' advanced placement class.

Lucky bitch, Kimberley thought.

Kimberley had also noticed that the archive on her phone was missing the one ace she could play against Bettina: a photo of the club's Top Mom, nude except for pearls and heels, while tethered to a spanking bench.

How had it disappeared?

The cell phone sales person assured her that if she found the old phone, it was likely still logged in its archive.

That does it, she vowed. I'm tearing the house apart the moment I get home.

She countered Jade's scowl with a supreme smile, then sauntered to the door after the others.

Lorna and Lily reached it at the same time. Kimberley held it open for them, but when Lorna walked through it, Kimberley murmured just loud enough for her to hear: "Fair warning: you're a fool to trust her."

Before Lorna could reply, Kimberley was already heading down the walkway. Still, she'd planted the seed.

But from the look on Lorna's face, she hadn't told her anything she hadn't already known.

Seeing Lorna and Lily heading their way, Jade held the elevator door for them.

"Wow, talk about like minds!" she exclaimed. "I hope you're right about blueberry being Bettina's favorite." She held it out for her friend to see.

"Yummy!" Lily exclaimed.

"What?" It took Lorna a moment for Jillian's words to register on her. "Oh! Sadly, I don't think Bettina will be in the mood to eat. Apparently, she just got"—remembering Lily's presence, she paused, then whispered, "R-A-I-D-E-D."

"Oh, my God," Ally murmured. "We thought Mallory and Sally's remarks were just their usual crazy paranoia."

Lorna grimaced. "Sadly, not this time. Look, maybe this isn't the best time to make a social call."

"If Bettina needs a show of support, now may be the best time of all," Ally pointed out.

"I guess you're right," Lorna conceded. "The way Kimberley was smirking, whatever is left of Bettina's reputation will be in shreds by this time next week."

"She'd better watch out. It's just as easy for her skeletons to make their way out of her closet," Jade muttered.

"Skeletons?" Lily wondered out loud. "Is that what she wants to be for Halloween?"

Everyone laughed uneasily.

Ally nudged Jade, and then whispered, "What exactly did you mean by that?"

Jade shrugged. "Nothing, just...forget it."

The elevator's chime told them they had reached their destination.

Jade's cryptic warning went out of Ally's mind when she saw the two U.S. Marshals who were blocking the front door.

"WHO ORDERED A PIE?" ONE OF THE MARSHALS SHOUTED down the hall.

"As, in pizza?" Another shouted back. "Bring it in. I could eat a horse."

"No, um..." Ally tried to think of a tactful way to put it: "This is a gift—for Mrs. Connaught Cross."

"Yo, Daniel!" the marshal shouted "There's a delivery at the door! Shouldn't we confiscate it too?" The man was practically salivating.

"What is it?" Daniel yelled back from somewhere on the second floor.

"A pie!" The man eyed it longingly.

"I don't eat pie!" Bettina's imperious declaration from above could be heard even at the front door.

"Well, the rest of us do," the marshal muttered.

"Okay, it's up for grabs," Daniel replied. "Get rid of the welcoming committee."

Jillian, Ally, and Jade exchanged relieved glances.

"Wait—we have Mrs. Connaught Cross's daughter with us." Lorna pointed to Lily. "This is an emergency. She must see her mother—*now*."

To help make their case, Jillian lifted the lid on the pie box. The smell of warm blueberries filled the hallway.

The man shrugged then yelled, "The Cross kid is here too. I'm sending her up."

"I'm the *Connaught* Cross kid," Lily corrected him.

"No, keep her downstairs!" Bettina declared.

To Lorna's ear, she sounded terrified. Why? What's happening up there? Lorna wondered.

"Send her up," Daniel commanded.

"Ladies, you'll find Mrs. *Connaught* Cross and Mr. *Daniel* Warwick in the master bedroom." The marshal gave Lily a smile and a wink.

He escorted them as far as the double circular staircase, but then headed off toward the kitchen with the pie.

The agents who passed them on the stairs were already making their way toward Bettina's formal dining room, with plates and forks.

"They better not leave crumbs on the table," Lily murmured.

Lorna thought it best not to point out that Bettina's problems were much bigger than pie crumbs—and for that matter, she wouldn't have ownership of her dining room table much longer anyway.

"Mummy…what *is* that?" Upon seeing the contents of her parents' closet, the look of horror on Lily's face matched the shock and awe in Lorna's, Jillian's, and Ally's eyes.

On the other hand, Jade thought, *Ah, so this was where Andy Hepburn took that nude photo of Bettina.*

Daniel Warwick turned to Lily. "You mean to say that you've never seen this closet?"

Her eyes narrowed as they shifted toward Bettina before gazing back to him. She shook her head slowly.

He crouched down, so that they were eye-to-eye. "Does either of your parents…well, what I mean to say is, have they ever hurt you?"

Frowning, she tilted her had to one side. "Are you asking if they spank me?"

"Yes." He smiled encouragingly. "It's okay. You can tell me the truth."

She snorted. "Now, that's silly! Why, I'm the best daughter in the world. Aren't I, Mummy?"

"But of course you are!" Bettina glared at Daniel, as if daring him to presume otherwise. She beckoned Lily to her side, but Lily was so in awe of the closet's contents that she didn't notice. Instead, she asked, "Mommy, did Daddy want to hurt you?"

Like Daniel, Lorna turned her head in embarrassment.

Oh. My God, Bettina thought. Now this man has me pegged as *a bottom*!

She opened her mouth to set him straight—until she saw the concern in his eyes.

She was the first one to glance away.

He turned to Lorna. "As of this moment, we have possession of Mrs. Connaught Cross's possessions, her home, and her automobile. She'll have to find somewhere else to live."

Lorna patted Bettina's arm. "Eleanor has already said that you and Lily can move in with her."

Bettina threw off her hand. "Lucky me." It annoyed Bettina that Hera had taken up residence in the two-room cabana house out by the pool. She turned to Daniel. "You can't leave me without a car! I'll need it to move my possessions." First on the list: the horse sculpture and its base.

"Sorry about that, but your car is now property of the U.S. Government. Perhaps your sister-in-law will be gracious enough to lend you hers." The arch in his brow dared her to ask Lorna.

"Bettina, you know I'd love to help, but Matthew took the car out this morning, and he's not answering his cell phone." Lorna winced. "And Eleanor is still up in Bolinas."

"But...but how will I carry my belongings out with me?" She could just see herself tottering on heels through Russian Hill with the horse sculpture's heavy base under her arm.

"Sorry," Daniel replied. "I guess you'll have to pack what you can in suitcases. I suggest taking any clothing purchased prior to two years ago, as well as any heirloom jewelry—"

She found some solace in the fact that she could at least hold on to her vintage couture collection, since the marshals would consider the dresses "old," as opposed to classic. "And...please, my daughter's art, in the dining room!" Bettina cast her eyes downward and bit her lip hard, to make herself cry.

One tear was the best she could do.

Apparently, it was all she needed. "Well...okay," Daniel replied grudgingly. "Point it out to me."

She practically ran down the staircase and into the dining room.

When Lorna and Daniel got there, she pointed to the sideboard. "There."

"She's quite a little artist." This time his smile was tender. "It'll take us a couple of days to inventory everything. Come back on Wednesday, before noon. I'll personally help you pack it into your mother's car."

"That is very sweet of you, Mr. Warwick...*Daniel*." This time when Bettina pursed her lips, it was to hide her smile.

Daniel walked out to the foyer, and yelled, "Okay, lunch break—everyone but Eddie. Eddie, you're to follow Mrs. Connaught Cross as she packs her final bag."

"But…what about lunch?"

"We'll bring you a doggie bag," Daniel assured him.

"But, I'm starving! Hey Daniel, do you mind if I have your piece of pie?"

Daniel shook his head in disgust. "Yeah, sure, whatever."

The rest of Daniel's crew followed him out the door.

LORNA WAITED UNTIL SHE HEARD THE FRONT DOOR SHUT before speaking. "Lily, would you mind giving me a few moments with your mother?" She tried to keep her voice calm, but she was so angry that she couldn't keep the tremor out of her voice.

Lily must have noticed because she scurried out the door and down the hall to her room.

Lorna waited until they no longer heard her footsteps before exploding. "My God, Bettina! You're into S&M?"

"My sex life is none of your business," Bettina hissed back. "Nor is it Eleanor's, by the way. If she finds out, I'll know who told her—and I'll make your life miserable for doing so."

"You mean even more miserable than you have already? Sure, okay, why stop now?"

"Ha! I knew it! You're going to run straight to Eleanor with my little indiscretion!"

Lorna pointed to the contents of the closet. "Little? Hardly! But you have nothing to worry about. Eleanor has enough on her mind already, what with trying to keep you out of prison." Livid that all Bettina could do was shrug, she added, "Oh, and by the way, we ran into your Top Moms posse in the lobby. They were practically chortling over your situation."

"Do tell," Bettina murmured, but Lorna knew she'd hit a nerve when her sister-in-law added, "That pack of bitches doesn't know how good they have it."

"Why did you invite them over, anyway?"

Bettina smiled supremely. "To clear the air. It's been six weeks since we last exchanged air kisses. I needed to show them I was still alive and kicking."

"As opposed to kicking and screaming in handcuffs?" Lorna shook her head in disbelief. "I wonder which one of your girlfriends tipped the Feds that you'd be preoccupied with company?"

Interesting theory—not that I'd let her know it, Bettina thought. Still, it's certainly something to investigate. "How do I know it wasn't you, as a way to embarrass me in front of my friends?" she countered.

"That's truly low, even for you!" Lorna stepped so close that they were nose-to-nose. "How would I have known, since I obviously wasn't invited, despite your promise to Eleanor to allow me to co-chair Top Mom committee meetings?"

Seeing Lorna's logic, Bettina scowled. "I presume Lily let the cat out of the bag."

"Well, you're wrong. Your daughter didn't sell you out." Bettina winced at the sadness in Lorna's voice.

"I've no doubt you'll do everything in your power to turn her against me!"

"Why would I, when you're quite capable of doing that yourself?"

"How dare you!"

"Someone *must* 'dare,' if not for you, then for Lily! And since I'm already in your crosshairs, I've got nothing to lose." Lorna grabbed tight to Bettina's wrist. "If you keep up your deceptions and accusations, she'll eventually see you as others do. Is that what you really want?"

"No! Of course not!… I mean"—Bettina trembled with anger at the accusation. "—I mean that, hopefully, her opinion of me won't be tainted by those who live to see me fail—such as yourself."

"Trust me, Bettina: I'm not the enemy." Lorna rolled her eyes. "Speaking of which, from the way your 'Top Moms' coterie were trash-talking you, I gather they got an eyeful of Dudley Do-Right and his SWAT team. Fair warning: those bitches are out to get you—all the more reason you shouldn't work so hard to alienate Jade, Ally, Jillian, and me."

"Why should I think any of them will trust me, after what I've done to them?" Bettina grumbled.

"Because they made a promise to Eleanor—and to me."

"How dare Mother! And how dare *you*!" Despite her declaration, Bettina was truly relieved to know their game plan.

So, Lorna and her friends want me to join their little entourage? Sure, okay, I'll play along, Bettina thought. *What have I got to lose? In fact, it might get me what I really want: Lorna, out of my club—and my life, once and for all.*

But for that, she'd need the one other dossier in the base: Lorna's.

2:22 p.m.

"I THOUGHT LILY AND YOU COULD SET UP IN HERE." Eleanor opened the larger of the three dormer windows in the room that had once been Bettina and Matthew's nursery. Besides the big playroom, the suite included two bedrooms and its own bath.

Bettina joined her at the window. Besides San Francisco Bay, it looked down on the pool and cabana house. Lorna's mother, Hera Harmony, her eyes closed, was standing on one foot in a Tai-Chi pose. She waved and smiled, almost as if she'd seen Bettina.

Bettina stepped back from the window, horrified.

"Lily will love it, what with the view of Angel Island. She'll hear the foghorns at night," noted Eleanor.

"I'll pass," Bettina sniffed.

Eleanor's smile faded. "I beg your pardon?"

"I'm sorry, Mother, but it also looks down onto the cabana house. The last thing I want to do is expose Lily to your hippie friend. I mean, my God—what if she's also a nudist?"

Eleanor rolled her eyes. "As it turns out, she is. But, so what? Live and let live, is what I say."

Bettina muttered, "Funny, you never said it when I was growing up."

"I did, but you chose to hear only what suited you."

"I'd rather we not fight, Mother. I've got a splitting headache as is, what with having to deal with that odious trustee, Mr. Warwick."

"Well, then, by all means, don't feel you have to stay here at all. Perhaps Matthew and Lorna will take you in." Eleanor started for the door.

"Mother, don't be ridiculous!" It was hard for Bettina to keep the panic out of her voice.

Her mother stopped and turned around. Seeing her mother's telltale show of anger—her left brow arched high in her forehead—Bettina murmured, "I mean…well, I certainly didn't mean to call you ridiculous."

"At least, that is to your benefit," Eleanor retorted. "You're always looking down your nose at others," Eleanor went on. "Your remark about Hera is a perfect example. Still, I'm your mother. I have to put up with it, even if others don't." She paused.

"If that's how you feel, I'll try to make it as painless as possible for you." Bettina retorted. "Lily and I will camp out downstairs, in the old servants' quarters. That way, we'll stay out of your way. "

"Suit yourself."

"Oh! Then, well...*fine.*" Bettina was somewhat disappointed that her mother wasn't going to beg her to reconsider. Noting her mother's frown, she added, "It's not as if Lily and I will be lurking in your basement forever. Once the judge in charge hears our attorneys and realizes I had no role in Art's mischief, my assets will be released to me, and things will go back to normal."

"Is that what you really want—for things to 'go back to normal'?"

"Yes, of course!"

"You disappoint me, Bettina. I never took you for a fool."

"I beg your pardon?"

"Art screwed you, and royally. He co-mingled your funds with his ill-gotten gains! A good forensic accountant will weed it out in no time—and believe me, the S.E.C. has an army of them."

"But...but...you never allowed him to get anywhere near my trust!"

"You're right. I've had your back since the day you accepted his marriage proposal. But, apparently, you didn't care enough to watch out for yourself."

"Mother, please! Quit talking in riddles." Bettina's headache felt like a gong was going off in her brain.

"Okay then, let me make this crystal clear. I don't know how he did it, but Art got your signature on a bank release form, giving him access to your checking account —the one where you draw your funds from the trustee account that your father set up in your name. In doing so, he not only put money in, he took it out."

"What?" Bettina closed her eyes to calm her heart that was pounding to the rhythm of her fear. "No! I'd never sign anything like that!"

"If you say so."

"Well, of course I say so!"

"That's exactly what I told our attorneys. But with last week's findings, it's highly unlikely that anyone is going to take you at your word."

"Why is that, Mother? What happened last week that can make this day any worse?"

"Despite your desire to pout, you've got to pull yourself together and listen to what I have to say," Eleanor warned her. "Things have gone from bad to worse. To help validate this to the Federal investigators, they had forensic and handwriting analyses conducted. Unfortunately, your fingerprints are all over the release form. Not only that, the handwriting expert verified it as your signature."

Bettina's knees buckled out from under her.

By the time Eleanor was at her side, she was back on her feet.

Angrily, Bettina waved her mother off. "Whether you believe me or not, I signed no such thing knowingly!"

"Too bad we can't prove it, my dear." It was the first time Bettina had heard defeat in her mother's voice.

Such irony. To think I was the one who brought her to this point.

"You'll find the bed sheets for the servants' wing in the laundry room."

Bettina was confused. "The…laundry room?"

"Downstairs. It's the door just before the servants' wing, so it should be easy to find."

"I know where to find the laundry room, Mother. I just presumed—"

"You presumed I was going to beg you to reconsider your guest quarters. Well, I'm not." Eleanor turned to the window, where, in all its glory, San Francisco Bay beckoned. "Others can walk away from you, Bettina, and have chosen to do so. As your mother, I cannot—and not just out of maternal love or familial duty, but because I truly do love you. I just hope that, someday, you'll give me reason to like you as well."

At this moment, Bettina wished that she, too, could walk away from what she'd created.

Her mother was right: she had no friends, and therefore nowhere else to go.

She headed downstairs to make her bed, and to lie in it.

CHAPTER FOUR

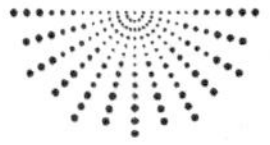

Tuesday, 3 September
9:05 a.m.

"You're late," Bettina muttered to Lorna.

"Only by eight minutes," Lorna retorted. She glanced over her sister-in-law's shoulder into the community room beyond. "So is everyone else, I see. Perhaps you should check your cell phone for text messages. With all the defections we've had lately, maybe your Top Moms decided to join the exodus."

Bettina shrugged. "Don't worry your pretty little head. They'll be here any moment now."

Because they had too much at stake. To remind them of this, late last night she placed her iPhone on a tripod. Setting it on selfie mode, she took photos of herself holding the statue in one hand and the recipient's file in the other.

Thank goodness, Eddie—the U.S. Marshal left to guard her at her house—was too busy chowing down on the pie to catch her doing it.

Today she had Eleanor's car with her. Right after the Top Moms Committee meeting, she'd head back over to the Summit in order to pick up the horse sculpture and its base. While she was there, she had to remember to pick up her cell phone charger. Sometime during the night, her phone battery died, and Eleanor's charger was incompatible.

When Eleanor suggested that she check to see if Hera had one, Bettina guffawed. "I doubt it, since she swears that cell phones are toxic to people and the environment. I presume she sends messages the old-fashioned way: by smoke signal."

Bettina began her morning by dropping Lily at her first day of kindergarten at the Pacific Heights Country Day School. The little girl was so excited about it that she woke Bettina before dawn. She was already dressed in her school's official uniform—a lavender gingham linen Dolce & Gabbana-designed shift, with a crisp white cotton Marc Jacobs blouse beneath it—and held her backpack at her side.

But, when Bettina pulled up to the school, Lily proclaimed, "No need to go in with me, Mother. I've already met my teacher. Remember? We were introduced at the school's Legacy Students Meet-and-Greet in May. She's very sweet, and allowed me to sit in the front row. I'll see you this afternoon at pick-up."

Before Bettina could protest, she hopped out of the car.

She doesn't want to be seen with me, she realized. Well, soon she'll be proud of me again.

For the first time in her life, Bettina's tears came easily.

After the Top Moms meeting, Bettina was going to grab the statue and its base, then head over to the school's "Trustee-Parent Welcoming Tea." Having whipped the Top Moms back into line, she was relying on Joanna Blunt to shield her from the sling and arrows of outrageous rumors that she somehow aided and abetted Art in his chicanery. For doing so, Joanna would be duly rewarded. Bettina would see to that, once she was safely ensconced on the school's trustee board.

Life wasn't perfect, but it certainly looked better now than it did just one day earlier.

Then again, before Labor Day, there was nowhere to go but up.

As she predicted, within the next five minutes the rest of the Top Moms had also grabbed a toddler-friendly chair around the circular kiddie table.

All were scowling except Jade. Good. The fact that Eleanor had successfully coerced both Lorna and the ditzy former pole dancer into being Bettina's new besties meant she'd have unwitting allies in her scheme to regain any power she may have lost, thanks to Art's imbecilic shenanigans.

She searched each face at the table, making eye contact until they at least acknowledged her tentative smile with a nod. Kimberley's arms were crossed, indicating some resistance, but only Mallory was stupid enough to frown crossly.

Bettina itched at the chance to make her pay for this public defiance, but now it was time for the honey. The vinegar would come later. "I want to thank you all for coming here today. It shows true strength of character and loyalty toward our friendships. Your trust today will not go unrewarded." She held out her hands to those on each side of her: Sally on one, and Kimberley on the other. "As a show of solidarity, please take my hand."

Not surprising, Sally did so without hesitation. On the other hand, Kimberley rolled her eyes before lightly laying her hand inside of Bettina's.

You'd think I'd just changed a diaper or something, Bettina thought. Gritting her teeth, she continued, "Now, Sally and Kimberley, if you'll place your other hand into the one of the person beside you—"

"What is this anyway, some sort of kumbaya?" Mallory groused.

"It's a demonstration of our solidarity," Bettina

snapped back. "The stronger we are as, er… *friends*, the stronger the club seems in the eyes of the public."

Reluctantly, Sally's hand went out to Mallory, who slapped her palm first, as if shaking off any cooties.

Lorna reached tentatively for Mallory's other hand. When Mallory cringed, she grabbed hold of it anyway. Lorna lucked out with her other hand. It went to Jade.

Kimberley tentatively held out her second hand to Jade, who blanched, then shuddered. Finally, when she took it, she grasped it so tightly that Bettina wondered when Kimberley was going to cry out, "UNCLE!"

Holding onto those poles must build up the muscles in your hands, Bettina reasoned.

Still, it was obvious that something had muddled the budding friendship between the two women. Not that it mattered to Bettina. Right now, she had only one agenda:

Total supremacy.

With that in mind, she followed Jade's lead, squeezing Kimberley's hand as hard as she could.

The redhead's tearful groan was music to her ears.

Time to slam down a velvet hammer on the rest of them too, metaphorically speaking. "Mallory. Sally. Kimberley. Jade"—she proclaimed, making eye contact with each in turn—"and now Lorna joins us in our quest for a fully experiential journey for our young children, and those of other women in Pacific Heights!" She tried her newfound skill at forcing a tear, but to no effect. Ah well, she'd have to wing it. "This year presents many challenges. Thank goodness for the club that each of you possesses a special skill that will help us accomplish this goal. For example, Sally's always-inquiring mind proves that you can never presume you've made your point. She is truly our idiot savant."

"You've got that right," Mallory snorted. "The first part, anyway."

Sally frowned. She knew she was being dissed... maybe? Sounded like it. Perhaps?

"And dear, dear Kimberley's loyalty to her fellow club members is second to none. We've all seen it in action." Bettina winked at Kimberley, who winked back, perhaps in order to clear the tears of pain from her eyes.

"As for Mallory, well..." Bettina paused in order to rearrange her lips into a smile, "she's certainly the club's 'Cassandra,' isn't she? And always fearsomely visceral in her predictions too."

"What the hell does that mean?" Belligerence pricked each word in Mallory's question.

"Back down, tiger! I'm paying you a compliment."

Mallory shrugged. "Oh! ...Well then, thanks...I guess."

"And what can I say about Jade that hasn't already been duly declared by others who know her even more intimately than any of us?"

"And isn't already written on the men's room wall at the Condor Club?" Mallory chortled.

Lorna held Jade's hand tightly, to prevent her friend from bitch-slapping Mallory.

Mission accomplished, Bettina thought. "Which brings me to Lorna." She turned to face her sister-in-law. "Everyone here knows we're family. You also know I've shown her no favoritism, but have allowed her to stand on her own merits"—she paused, then added, "—and I think you'll agree with me that she has competently done so."

Her gaze dared anyone to disagree with her.

No one was foolish enough to do so.

Still, there is one more test that ensured total supremacy: "I could rhapsodize forever on the joys of friendship—"

"Please don't," Mallory groaned.

Bettina glared at her. "But, as Mallory just pointed out, time is of the essence, and we must get on with club business." She let go of Kimberley's hand in order to grab the file folders that lay in front of her.

"Truly...inspirational," Kimberley gasped. She flinched as she attempted to shake the pain from her hand. Jade too released the other wrist—thankfully, still in one piece. But her scowl promised payback in the not-so-distant future.

Bettina smiled. *Catfight! Meow...*

She handed each woman a folder with the club's admission submissions. "Let's start by filling in the slots left by the defections." She rolled her eyes. "The nerve of some people, walking away from the club in its time of need! Well, good riddance to bad rubbish—"

"Hear, hear!" Mallory seconded her. "If you can't take the heat, get out of the kit—"

"Yada, yada, okay, everyone gets the picture," Bettina assured her. "I presume each of you did as I asked, and have your Onesies top picks? …Good! Mallory, why don't you start with—"

Lorna raised her hand. "Um…I hate to interrupt, Bettina, but I think you forgot something."

How dare she interrupt me, Bettina thought. Keep your cool—

But nip it in the bud—*NOW*. "Yes, what is it, Lorna?" Exasperation dripped thickly off each honeyed syllable.

"You'll want to let the rest of the Top Moms know that I'll be joining you as co-Chief Executive Mom of the Pacific Heights Moms & Tots Club."

Dead silence.

Until Mallory snorted.

Bettina's silence elicited a gasp from Sally.

Too late, Kimberley swallowed her sneer.

None of this was lost on Bettina. She lowered her hands below the table so that the others could not see how tightly her fists were clenched. When she found her voice again, she calmly replied, "We'll do everything we can to make your sacrifice a memorable one."

Sacrifice?

That sounds ominous, Lorna thought.

Jade must have thought so too, because her eyes widened with concern.

Bettina smells fear. Stay calm. Lorna forced her lips into a grin. "Thank you, Bettina! You don't know how much that means to me!" She reached over and patted Bettina's hand. "The Top Moms Committee does an admirable job, and shoulders more than its fair share of responsibility. Everyone is aware of that."

Bettina's eyes narrowed. Had she opened her mouth, Lorna would not have been surprised to see fangs. She shook the fantasy from her mind, and continued: "So, why not take advantage of the club's most natural resources of all—its mothers?"

"We do everything we can to take advantage of them already," Mallory pointed out.

"She means, metaphorically speaking," Bettina clarified.

Not that anyone was fooled. Still, Lorna felt it best to ignore the obvious. "We have a very deep bench of women who are used to responsibility. The club has been good to them. It has taught their children to socialize, and to play fairly. And it has introduced both children and mothers to lifelong friends. We've helped them invest in their futures. So, why not set up an infrastructure to allow them to give back to our wonderful organization?"

Bettina frowned. "And just exactly how will this payback occur?"

"Why not start by devising a fairer division of duties?" Lorna opened her bag and pulled out a sheaf of papers. She handed out one to each of them. "This is just a rough idea of how we can spread the wealth, as it were."

Jade gave a whistle. "It's a full schematic, outlining every week—"

"And utilizing every mom, but only with two tasks a year," Sally murmured. "Awesome!" She slapped her hand over her mouth when she realized she said that out loud.

Suspicious, Kimberley asked, "But how could that be? …Wait, from what I'm seeing here, you want to double the size of the club!"

"We have more applications than we can accept, so why not?" Lorna countered.

Mallory rolled her eyes. "Because adding more families will make PHM&T *less exclusive*."

"Not necessarily. It means more people will spread the word about how great it is," Jade pointed out. "And, considering the bad press we've gotten lately, maybe that's not such a bad thing."

Kimberley shrugged. "On the bright side, it will certainly up the anxiety level to know that, even with more slots, you still may not make it into the club."

"Hey, this chart shows four Top Moms for each age group!" Mallory cried out.

Lorna nodded. "With bigger groups, it makes sense."

Adamantly, Mallory shook her head. "It would *never* work!"

"Sure it would," Lorna said evenly. "Four means less burnout, more shared responsibilities, and Bettina or I can weigh in if a tie-breaker is needed."

"You mean, so that you can side with the new Top Moms," Kimberley muttered.

"You're presuming that you and the Top Moms in your group won't become even closer. You will, though, because you'll spend managing your tasks together. Jade, Ally, Jillian, and I are proof that you're wrong."

Kimberley started to say something, then thought it better to keep her mouth shut.

Whatever she did to lose Jade as a friend must be a doozy, Lorna thought. "Which brings me the last item on my agenda. I'd like to recommend a change in our selection process." Lorna cupped her hands. "So that it's fair and square, we should do it as an open lottery."

"Are you kidding?" Mallory exploded. She turned to Bettina. *"Is she kidding?"*

"Why is that so bad?" Sally asked. "We don't need even *more* people hating us."

"This is nonsense," Mallory insisted. "The next thing we know, you'll want to open it up to single moms, and working moms too."

"As long as they're able to attend the majority of the meet-ups, and carry out their assigned tasks, then sure, why not?" Lorna declared. The thought that Ally and Jillian were perfect examples of it put a slight smile on her lips. "In fact, there should be some input from the member body, as a whole, on some of the more important rules and regulations that affect their participation."

Kimberley, Sally, and Mallory gasped.

All eyes turned to Bettina.

She said nothing. Then, finally: "Ladies, why don't we put it to a vote? All those in favor of the status quo, please raise your hands?"

Mallory and Kimberley's hands went up. Reluctantly, Sally's did too.

Bettina nodded. "And those against it?"

Jade and Lorna raised their hands.

Bettina sighed.

Then, she raised her hand.

Jade looked around. "We have a tie. Should we vote again?"

"It's not necessary," Bettina retorted. "Under the club's bylaws, the Chief Executive Mom's vote is also the tiebreaker. Ladies, we are now in an era of a kinder, gentler Pacific Heights Moms & Tots Club."

One can only hope, Lorna thought.

Bettina turned to Kimberley. "You and Jade have the task of writing up the name of each candidate on a Post-It Note, by group, for the drawing."

Jade and Kimberley recoiled in unison.

Bettina continued, "The drawing will take place here,

tomorrow, at nine-fifteen sharp. Please make the necessary arrangements for *die kinder*."

Mallory stalked out. Kimberley was close at her heels.

Sally waved tentatively at the others, but nonetheless stumbled out after them.

"Oh! So, I guess my vote counted twice too," Lorna murmured.

Noting the look of hate on Bettina's face, she wished she'd kept her mouth shut.

"HAS JILLIAN BEEN ABLE TO TALK ALLY INTO RE-APPLYING?" Lorna asked.

Jade shook her head. "Ally uses the excuse that she wants to focus on V.C. funding for Life of Pie, and of course, Brady."

Lorna patted Jade's hand. "Have they finally moved in together?"

This time, Jade nodded. "Yes, into Brady's house, since it's the larger of the two homes. Right now, they're using her townhome as an office, but her pal, Barry, wants to buy her half of the duplex." Not only was Barry Simon Ally's oldest and dearest friend, and her attorney, he was Zoe's biological father. He and his partner, Christian Cordell, doted on the little girl.

"Darn it." Lorna frowned. "We've got to get her to

change her mind between now and tomorrow, when the lottery takes place."

Jade smiled slyly. "No, we don't. All we have to do is make sure that her application is in the pile, and that her name is one of those being drawn."

Lorna's eyes grew large. "Jade…you wouldn't—would you?"

"Heck yeah, I would! And since I was instructed to make the lottery name slips, no one will be any wiser. Besides, you and I both know that the club won't be the same without her." Considering her role in getting Ally exiled in the first place, she meant that from the bottom of her heart.

Lorna winked at her friend. "I'll pretend I didn't hear you say that."

"Fine by me. Just be sure to pull her name. In fact, I'll slip it to you right before it's your turn to draw."

Oh, my God, she thought, I'm just as devious as Bettina!

She consoled herself with one thing: everything she was doing was with the objective of lightening Bettina's load, and living up to her promise to Eleanor.

She couldn't wait to tell Eleanor how well the meeting went.

But first things first: get home and find out what was really happening with Matt.

CHAPTER FIVE

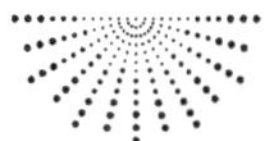

10:13 a.m.

BETTINA GOT TO THE SUMMIT JUST AS THE LAST OF HER possessions were being loaded onto a moving van.

She rushed up to the man who seemed to be in charge. "My daughter's artwork! It wasn't supposed to leave the premises. Daniel Warwick promised!"

He nodded. "Not to worry, Mrs. Cross. It's right where you left it. In fact, Mr. Warwick is up there now. He'll lock up the moment you take it."

"Oh…good. Thank you." She hurried inside.

THE FRONT DOORS WERE LOCKED.

A realtor's combination key lock box hung from one of the handles.

Bettina shoved her hand into a pocket of her purse until she found her keys. She tried the key in the lock, but it didn't work.

Son of a bitch, she thought. The Feds already changed it!

She stifled the urge to bang on the door. Instead, she rang the bell. It was chosen because its chimes replicated that of Westminster, which seemed to scare the bejeezus out of everyone.

Ah, good times. Alas, no more.

A moment later, the doors swung open. Daniel gazed down at her. "Mrs. Connaught Cross! Just in time."

He stepped aside so that she might enter, all the while keeping his eyes on her.

She felt herself blushing. "Thank you for keeping your promise about my daughter's artwork." She held out her hand to him.

He grasped it firmly. She hadn't expect it to envelope hers so fully, or to be so warm.

She couldn't understand why she was disappointed when his hand dropped away. "Shall we?"

She nodded. She looked up and around. The two-story foyer was now devoid of all its furnishings. Its naked walls were marred with the ghostly shadows of the framed artwork that once hung there.

As she made her way toward the dining room, the sharp click of her heels reverberated through the empty marble foyer. The sound made her angry.

Most of all, she was scared.

Perhaps she was also foolish to think that she could ever recover the respect and prestige she once had.

In truth, had she really had it?

The thought that it had all been an illusion—a silly presumption built on her own pettiness and a need to attain respect from her mother—hammered her harder than any headache.

It struck her that she'd seen more tenderness and concern from Eleanor since Art's debacle than during the thirty-three years that came before it.

Such irony.

Is that it—my mother can only love losers? Ah! So, that's why Matt has always been her favorite.

Bettina abhorred what she deemed as her brother's laziness. She loathed him for his lack of desire to do anything to change it.

To her way of thinking, it was nobler to be driven, even if one was despised by everyone else for being so.

If I'm hated, then so be it.

"After you, Daniel," she purred demurely.

"Is this some kind of joke?" Bettina could not believe her eyes.

The only things left in the dining room were the four watercolors that had hung over the sideboard.

The sideboard itself was gone, as was the horse sculpture and its base.

Daniel stared at her, then at the wall, and back to her. "What are you talking about? The pictures are right there."

"I didn't mean the pictures!" Bettina's heart was beating so quickly that she could only gasp.

"You mean to tell me that this *isn't* your daughter's artwork?"

"Of course it is!"

Daniel frowned. "Mrs. Connaught Cross, perhaps you can enlighten me as to where I've failed you."

"I meant—the *horse sculpture!*"

He crossed his arms at his chest. "You mean to tell me that the horse was also made by Lily?"

"Yes...*yes!*" She willed herself to look him straight in the eye. Could he tell she was lying? She couldn't fathom his thoughts behind those startling gray eyes.

"Lily...will be heartbroken," she gasped. "Please, you must help me get it back!"

He shrugged. "It's already in the warehouse, and therefore it's the property of the court. The auction is to take place early next year—"

"So, there is still time to get it back before it's sold!" Bettina's hand flew to his chest. "Please…"

His heart picked up its pace.

Still, he didn't shake off her palm.

The flush in her cheeks signaled him that she knew she should remove it.

And yet, she didn't.

If his hand had been on her breast, he would have felt her heart racing too.

Finally, he said, "There will need to be some quid pro quo."

She frowned. "I see." He's just like all the others, she thought. Oh, well. If this was to be a business proposition, there was no need to flirt. She let her hand fall to her side. "What do you have in mind?" she asked, as if she didn't already know.

Hell, he's seen my closet, she reasoned. I guess he presumes anything goes.

"Let me buy you a late lunch, tomorrow. We'll talk then. Shall I pick you up at, say, one-thirty?"

She was confused. "But…Is that allowed?"

"Talking?" He grinned. "Sure. In fact, the court encourages it." He plucked two of Lily's frames off the wall, then the other two. "Let me walk these down to the car for you."

He steered her back into the foyer, then out the door.

This is the last time I'll be in my house, she realized. I should be sad.

But she wasn't.

In truth, she was relieved. It was as if a boulder had been lifted off her shoulders. Her life was moving in a new direction.

She was afraid of where it would lead her.

AFTER LEAVING DANIEL, BETTINA WENT BACK TO ELEANOR'S house. Her mother was nowhere to be found, nor was Hera, thank goodness.

She went through the items of wardrobe salvaged from her home invasion, and finally chose a seventeen-hundred-dollar Peter Pilotto abstract print sheath.

Next stop: the library of the Pacific Heights Country Day School. Bettina had long dreamed of this day: attending the Trustee-Parent luncheon on her daughter's first day of school, just as Eleanor had done for her, and Eleanor's mother, Grandmother Morrow, had done for Eleanor.

She planned on arriving a few minutes late, but that was on purpose. Bettina was ready to turn heads, but this time for all the right reasons.

Because she belonged.

2:00 p.m.

"I'M SORRY—WHO ARE YOU AGAIN?" THE PACIFIC HEIGHTS Day School volunteer mother perused the guest list in front of her for the second time. "Connaught, did you say?"

"Yes...Well, perhaps it's under, um, Cross," Bettina muttered. Her husband's surname stuck in her throat.

"Cross?" The woman looked up. "Oh! ...Um..." She pursed her lips.

"Is something wrong?" Bettina asked. Just then, Bettina noticed Joanna Blunt. The former Top Mom was standing at the head table with some of the Trustees. Like them, she wore a yellow rose corsage.

Why, that lucky ducky, thought Bettina. She was chosen to represent as this year's parent trustee! Good, then she's perfectly placed to help me with damage control—

The check-in volunteer tugged on Bettina's sleeve in order to get her attention. "I'm sorry, ma'am, but you're not on the list. Perhaps if you can step to one side." She turned to the mother behind Bettina, and motioned her forward.

Bettina stood her ground. "Impossible! I am a legacy. My mother is a legacy, and her mother was a legacy! Needless to say, I am on your list."

The woman glanced to the side and nodded slightly at a security guard.

What the hell is going on here? "My daughter spent all day today in Ms. Coleman's kindergarten class— "

"No, Bettina, she didn't." Bettina recognized the voice coming from behind her. She turned around to face the Head of School, Brad Pickering.

Despite having been part of the head-of-school selection committee that chose him to replace the last headmaster, Bettina did not particularly like him. He was too tall and too thin, practically a live cadaver. Surely he scared the children too.

No matter. During the interview Mr. Pickering was properly obsequious. To know one's place was always appreciated by Bettina. A sycophantic demeanor would do, toadying was the ideal. He showed the chops. It was why she'd voted for Pickering in the first place.

But, now there was an imperious air about him, almost as if he actually ran the place.

As if.

But Bettina didn't have time to deal with it today. "Mr. Pickering, what do you mean when you said that Lily wasn't in Mrs. Coleman's class? Did she get reassigned to another teacher?"

He grimaced. "No. She's been sitting in my office all day."

"*Why*? What happened?"

"Had you picked up your cell phone, you might have known."

She winced at his chiding. *Damn it! I forgot to get my cell phone charger.*

"Perhaps we should join Lily. She's waiting for you in my office." He nodded down the widest of the school's hallowed halls.

As they walked, Pickering stayed at her side, but there was no fawning over her as in the past, and no ingratiating smile on his lips.

When they entered his office, his secretary's smile faded when she noticed Bettina with him.

When he opened the door, Lily was in plain sight, sitting on his couch. Her eyes were damp and red-rimmed. She looked up, but she didn't run to her mother.

In fact, she turned her head to the window.

Oh, my God, Bettina thought. She hates me too.

The realization broke Bettina's heart.

"WHY ISN'T MY DAUGHTER IN HER CLASSROOM?" BETTINA demanded.

Mr. Pickering shrugged. "Because she is no longer enrolled here."

Bettina could not believe her ears. "Are you delirious? There have been Morrows and Connaughts enrolled in Pacific Heights Country Day School for over one hundred years! Since it's first graduating class, I might add!"

"Which makes it a greater shame that this generation of the Morrow and Connaught bloodline will be doing without the honor of gracing our halls." Mr. Pickering's tone was meant to indicate that there was to be no further discussion on the issue.

To hell with that.

"Why, pray tell, are we being denied our legacy rights?" Bettina snarled.

"Sadly, Lily is a victim of your husband's unfortunate circumstances. Paragraph fifteen, subparagraph A, the document of the school's contract that you signed as part of the application process for dear sweet Lily clearly states that any payment made with the use of illicit funds will result in immediate dismissal of the student—*and* the forfeiture of any prepaid tuition." He walked over to his desk, and perused it for the referenced section. Finding it, he handed it to her.

She snatched it out of his hand. "The funds were not ill-gotten. They came from my trust—which, by the way, has paid for at least three generations of alumni," Bettina pointed out.

"Were that the only clause in question, the school's trustee board might have actually reconsidered poor little Lily's plight. However, it wasn't the only clause broken." His bony finger pointed to the contract's clause number twenty-two. "As you see here, quote, students, or their parents who have been tainted with some form of public disgrace will result in the immediate expulsion of said student, end-quote." His claw-like hands fluttered open, as if her daughter's fate was out of his hands.

"My husband has yet to go to trial," Bettina countered.

"Only because he is, as ruffians are keen to say, 'on the lam.'" Mr. Pickering clucked his tongue in disdain.

"Do you know how much Pacific Heights Country Day School has benefited from the Morrow and Connaught largesse?"

"The exact accounting has been put at over fourteen million six hundred and seventy-two thousand dollars and change." He winced. "Your family's generosity will not be overlooked; the school's new library will one day carry the Morrow Connaught name again..." He paused, and added, "...but perhaps we should skip a generation. You know, wait until things cool down."

"I presume I'll get a refund on the hefty pre-paid tuition. And let's not forget her very expensive uniforms—"

He shook his head. "Alas, no. All sales are final."

"If that's the case, my family's generosity can, and will, be withdrawn," Bettina warned. "I presume my mother is not yet aware that her alma mater and pet beneficiary has shown her granddaughter the door."

He blanched. "No, of course not! We felt it best that she hear it from you."

"Cowards!"

"Please, Mrs. Connaught Cross, no need to stoop to name-calling!"

"And to believe it was my vote that served as the tiebreaker that rewarded you with this very position you now hold," she hissed.

Mr. Pickering patted down the sweat on his bald pate with his handkerchief. "Mrs. Connaught Cross, I'm am quite aware of that, and have thanked you profusely on numerous occasions."

She stepped in, menacingly. "So, why stop genu-flecting now? You know what they say: one good deed deserves another."

"Believe me, Mrs. Connaught Cross, I would give anything to have the whole matter forgotten! Between the loss of your patronage and that of your mother's—well, let's just say our fundraising efforts will be sorely tested." By now his hankie was so wet that he had to reach into his desk for another. "But, let's not forget that several trustees were, in fact, victims of your husband's duplicity. Perhaps Lily's admission would have gone unnoticed, had not one in particular been aware of it."

"How could that be? There are at least three hundred students in the school, and thirty-six new students in this year's kindergarten alone. Who on the trustee board would have even been aware of Lily's admission...?" Her voice faded away when she realized she already had the answer:

Joanna Blunt.

Joanna was at the house when Daniel and his SWAT team raided it. She overheard him say that all of Bettina's possessions were to be auctioned off.

Perhaps she planned on buying the sculpture and its base herself!

I have to get it back at all costs. That way, I'll have the leverage to convince Joanna to rally behind Lily's readmission.

Without another word, she hustled Lily out the door.

CHAPTER SIX

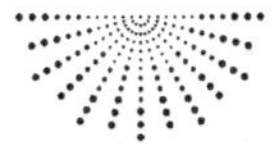

5:24 p.m.

"You should have seen the look on Bettina's face when Pickering unceremoniously hustled her out of the library. Priceless!" Joanna's giggles were contagious.

Mallory followed it with a roaring guffaw of her own. Kimberley's way of reveling in their success was to smile slyly, raise her glass, and offer a toast. "Here's to getting rid of that bitch, once and for all."

The bartenders at Jardinière were used to tipsy ladies during the bar's happy hour, and these tipsy ladies in particular—especially the redhead with the roaming hands, who didn't need happy hour as an excuse to tipple, or worse, to be hands-on with them. Invariably, the bartenders flipped a coin to see who served her, which meant getting within groping distance. At least her tips were always worth it—that is, until recently.

Thus, the dearth of service today.

Joanna clinked Kimberley's glass. "How perfectly delicious that the U.S. Marshals planned their raid during our meeting!"

Kimberley snorted so hard that champagne came out through her nose. "What…you think that was some sort of kismet? Ha! Hardly. I figured it was time that the barbarians got a little help climbing Queen Bettina's castle walls. I tipped off that Warwick hottie about our meeting, and then made sure that the door was conveniently left open. The rest is history."

Her offer was made over the phone. Had Kimberley known he was such a hunk, she would have sought him out in person. Perhaps he would have given her a reward or something. Not that it could have made up for all the money Jerry lost by investing with Art.

She would have settled for something other than cash —say, a roll in the hay.

"My, my, aren't you a clever one!" Mallory slapped Kimberley on the back. Unfortunately, what was left in her glass spilled all over the marble countertop. "Watch it, Mallory! My God, you don't know your own strength. My next drink is on you." And, the sooner the better.

"I can't believe Bettina smuggled out our dossiers, right out from under the nose of the Federal trustee," Joanna groused. "When she sent that text of the picture of her, holding my file, I just about had a cow. And, of course, I erased it immediately! Ever since I confronted Frank about his…well, his indiscretion, he's so worried I'll divorce him and take him for every dime that he's been on the defensive. The last thing I needed to let him know was where I got the information. Hell, he might pay Bettina for a copy of the file just to keep it out of my hands—"

Kimberley was too thirsty to listen to her chatter. Unfortunately, both of the bartenders were down at the far ends of the horseshoe-shaped bar. One was hovering over a couple that looked familiar. Kimberley's jaw dropped open when she realized who they were. The woman was Kelly Overton—one of last year's probationary Onesies, who, rumor had it, was exiled for somehow besting Bettina in some way. The man she was flirting with was Andy Hepburn, the British soccer coach hired to teach the sport to last year's Twosies. He'd been the wet dream of every Twosie mom.

Andy had been more than that to Kimberley: the dominant in their somewhat painful, albeit always pleasurable, relationship—

Until he chose Bettina to replace her.

"*Oh. My. God,*" Kimberley murmured.

Mesmerized, Kimberley elbowed Joanna, causing the stately brunette to tilt her white wine onto her purse.

"What the hell?" Joanna yelped. "You soaked my new Fendi!" She shoved back, hard.

This time, Kimberley fell onto Mallory.

Mallory was smart enough to sidle away just in the nick of time, but she too was shocked at what she saw. "Well, what do you know!" She downed her straight scotch in a gulp. "I guess that answers the question on everyone's mind."

"Oh yeah? What's that?" Joanna asked, but like the others, she was too dumbstruck to look away.

Mallory winked knowingly. "Whether Andy is gay."

Joanna and Kimberley's heads whipped around to stare at her. "What?" They exclaimed in unison. Then, again, together: "*As if!*"

Realizing their mutual assessment, they burst out laughing.

Now it was their turn to be stared at, by everyone in the bar, including Andy and Kelly.

Kimberley froze, like a deer in the headlights of an eighteen-wheeler.

The couple waved at them. Then they kissed, as if they were the only people in the room.

Kimberley felt nauseous. Well, at least Andy had moved on from Bettina.

Mallory smirked, "Well, well, well. I wonder what Bettina would think of that?"

"Good question," Joanna mused. "An even better one is, 'what happened between Kelly and Bettina?'"

Suddenly, Kimberley had a great idea. "There's only one way to find out. Why don't we ask her?"

"Who, Bettina?" Mallory guffawed. "She'd never tell us. *She doesn't trust us.*"

"No, you idiots. I meant, why don't we ask Kelly what really happened to get her kicked out of the club?" She nodded toward the other side of the bar. "Maybe she'd spill the beans as to why Bettina turned on her right before we voted on the final four Onesie Moms."

Joanna shook her head. "Nah. I mean, come on. Would *you*?"

"Kelly was smart to get out when she did," Mallory pointed out. "Whereas, the rest of us are going down with the Good Ship PHM&T."

"Oh, I don't know." Kimberley shrugged. "Maybe Kelly wouldn't mind a comeback. And more so, if Bettina goes down the way we think she will—"

"You mean, in handcuffs and leg-irons?" Mallory chortled. "That's wishful thinking on your part."

"You're right. Besides, she'd probably like it," Kimberley muttered. "What I'm trying to say is that we'll need allies in the club, now more than ever, if we're to stop Lorna from having her way and making the application selection a free-for-all. So, why don't we ask Kelly to re-apply?"

Joanna downed her drink. "If you want to make that your own personal project, go for it. As for me, I have to get home and relieve the babysitter." She snapped her fingers at Mallory. "Fair warning: since your little brat has been terrorizing my sitter since the moment she stepped into my house, I think you'll need to lay a better tip on her. I can't afford to lose another one."

"My God, I don't see why everyone freaks out because Ferguson is a little rambunctious!" Mallory bemoaned. "He's just all boy."

"No, he's 'all brat'," Joanna retorted. "And it's time you face up to it before you're bailing him out of S.F. Juvee Detention every other day."

Mallory tossed down the cash needed to pay for their drinks. "No, he isn't—and, no, I won't! If anything, he'll be a white-collar criminal, and pardoned by the best president money can buy—which is any president in office at the time."

Joanna air-kissed Kimberley. "Aren't you walking out with us?"

Kimberley shook her head. "Tiny bladder. Got to hit the ladies' room."

She waved to them until they were out the door.

Then she turned, and smiled sweetly at Kelly.

Kelly smiled back.

Andy frowned.

I guess he thinks I'll tell her how she can expect to be treated as his latest conquest.

Kimberley's grin grew even bigger at the thought.

Well, he's right.

"Did you enjoy fucking her?" Kelly asked Andy as Kimberley made her way over to them.

"I enjoyed shagging them all." After three beers, his Mancurian accent was thicker than ever.

A few stout ales had a way of thickening his dick too, she'd noticed.

"But of course you did, darling." Kelly made sure that their kiss took as long as Kimberley's stroll to their end of the bar.

Kelly had first met Andy at Good Vibrations, the sexual apparel shop on Polk Street. Both were admiring a particular flogger called "the Terminator."

"You look as if you could stand up to it," he teased her.

"You'd fold like a deck of used Vegas poker cards," she teased back.

"Ah…right you are." He clucked his tongue when he realized that she, like him, felt it was more blessed to give than to receive.

Soon they noticed each other at the many private BDSM gatherings that catered to the pleasures they sought. He was curious enough about her to seek her out as she did her thing: playing kitten with a whip, while trussed up in patent leather and thigh-high boots. She did the same with him, watching how he wooed his subs with naughty talk and gentle smacks before the rough stuff had them sobbing into their ball gags.

Usually, for more of the same.

After one party in the spring—the annual "Break My Heart, You Brazen Tart" extravaganza, held at Kink.com's headquarters at the Mission Armory—they met for drinks afterward, in order to relive the high points, and to critique each other's technique.

"Your last sub was achin' for the lash." Andy rewarded her with a grudging wink. "You certainly gave him what for."

"Your bottom could have used a little finesse," she'd countered. "Do you really like it when the sluts squeal like little piggies?"

By the end of the summer, by mutual consent, they had sex.

It was a disaster. It may take two to tango, but only one can lead in any dance.

But, then Kelly came up with a brilliant idea: "Let's meet every couple of weeks or so. We'll bring a sub or two, and watch each other do our thing. Then, if the mood strikes…"

Boy, did it ever.

"Brilliant," Andy gasped after his first orgasm during their first trial run.

It was not to be his last.

In some respect, they were a couple. If the mood suited them, they'd widen their lovefest to a throuple, but it rarely did. Both were too jealous to share their intimacy with anyone else.

As Kimberley made her way toward them, Kelly

murmured, "What did you ever see in her?"

He thought for a moment, and then muttered, "She'd do anything I asked."

Good to know, Kelly thought. If she wants to play with us, she'll have to do anything I ask too.

When they were finally face to face, Kimberley began with some polite chatter, along the lines of, "Long time, no see...," and "Imagine running into both of you, and together, no less...," and "Wow, so much has happened in the meantime..."

Months ago, Kelly and Andy established the perfect shorthand for just such occasions: a subtle wink, then, if the prospect were a man, Kelly would assert the necessary pressure on the right appendage. If it was a woman, Andy was all hands: tender touches, not so subtle pats, and if any of the precursory moves lit a fire behind her wary eyes, an outright grope.

From the look in her eyes, Kimberley was on fire even before Andy's first stroke.

This is much too easy, Kelly thought.

5:53 p.m.

THE HOLIDAY INN WAS JUST A FEW BLOCKS UP, ON VAN NESS Avenue. It wasn't exactly a romantic setting, but it was quick and convenient for the two women, both who had less than an hour to relieve their babysitters.

Kelly and Andy checked in first, as a couple. When they got into the room, Kelly called Kimberley's cell phone with the room number.

Ten minutes later, she sauntered into the lobby as if she owned the place. The front desk clerk was too busy directing a couple of German tourists to the nearby SF Jazz Center to notice her.

However, the dental supply salesman whose bedroom shared a wall with theirs was quite aware of her, what with all the ecstatic moans coming from their bedroom. He had no issue with it. Hell, it was much better than porn for his personal needs.

When the rough stuff started, his initial disappointment was that it brought him to climax too soon.

As Kimberley's yelps got louder and came faster, he wondered if he should intervene, and not just because his first appointment was at the crack of dawn.

Okay, yeah, that was the driving motivation.

Had her ecstatic grunts gone on longer than an hour, he would have called the front desk. At least, that's what he told himself.

That night, he slept like a baby.

I'VE MISSED YOU, ANDY.

Had he not crammed the ball gag into Kimberley's mouth the moment she entered the room, she would have made sure to tell him.

Instead, she'd have to let her body language speak for her.

In other words, she took her beating like a pro.

"Impressive," Kelly murmured approvingly.

But, Kimberley hated when Kelly took her turn with the lash. "Payback is a bitch, ain't it?" Kelly cooed in her ear. "So naughty of you to vote against me."

With the gag in her mouth, Kimberley's words came out garbled, but Kelly got the gist of it. *"OUCH!—I didn't; I swear!—OUCH! OUCH!* I voted against Jade! Fuck! That *HURT!"*

Kelly let loose with a throaty chuckle. "Then I'll be lenient on you—*next time."* She tossed down the whip.

"Wait…that's it?"

Kelly examined a broken nail. "Why? What else did you expect?"

Kimberley turned to Andy. "I thought we'd…well, you know."

"Feck? Is that what you're trying to say?" His grin encouraged her to nod.

Kelly laughed. "Sorry, honey. You've had your fun. It's my turn now." Her smile disappeared. "Go home and play mommy dearest."

Kimberley was livid. She'd never done a threesome before. Sure, they were popular while she was in college, but the thought of having another woman's hands and mouth roaming over her body had never appealed to her —sort of like being forced to eat an appetizer that turned your stomach before getting to the main course that had you salivating.

In this case, the prime beefcake was known as "Randy" Andy Hepburn.

There he stood: ready, willing, and hardened. But he was Kelly's just desserts, not hers.

All the more reason to get Kelly back into the club. The more she saw of Kelly, the more she'd see of Andy.

And if I play my cards right, Kelly will be too busy jousting with Bettina to notice that Andy's attentions had shifted to me.

Kelly snapped her fingers at Andy as the command to unbind their sub.

Kimberley held out her hands to him. Instinctively, their eyes met.

His sly wink was all she needed to know her plan would work.

Now that the bindings were loosened, Kimberley rubbed the rawness from her wrists. "Kelly, please—there's something I want to ask you."

Kelly sighed as she pulled her blouse from her skirt. "What the hell is it?"

"I...I think you should reapply to PHM&T." There, she'd said it.

Kelly was laughing so hard that she almost tore a

button from her blouse. "Oh, yeah? And why would I do that?"

"Because…because we've changed the admission policy. You won't have to worry about Bettina's little sadistic trials, or anything like that. And—well, I'd make sure you'd get in."

"Just why would I want back in, anyway? The reputation of your little club was smeared along with Bettina's, remember?" Kelly unsnapped her bra.

Embarrassed, Kimberley looked away. "Don't you want to be there when Bettina is finally voted out?"

She didn't have to look at Kelly's face to imagine the smirk on it.

"Okay, sure, I'll put in for the club." Kelly scooped Kimberley's Louboutins off the floor and tossed one to her. "But if I go through the process of applying and I don't get in, do you know what I'll do to you?"

Kimberley bit her lip. "I…I think I can imagine."

The other shoe hit Kimberley on the forehead. "No, you can't," Kelly muttered. "Now get the hell out of here."

Shoes in hand, Kimberley stumbled out of the room.

Kelly turned to Andy. "You better not be soft," she growled.

He laughed. "After that conversation? Bloody hell, I'm the fecking Rock of Gibraltar!"

For once, it was more than a boast.

6:55 p.m.

Jade immediately discovered one downside to having Reggie fully and gainfully employed:

He wasn't around for her to talk to.

And right now, she needed someone to grouse over the issue of having to work with Kimberley in putting together the lottery names.

All day long she avoided picking up Kimberley's calls, let alone calling her back. But now that the housework was done and Oliver was tucked into bed, the time had come for her to deal with the task, one way or the other.

She looked at her watch. Reggie had stayed in Berkeley to attend a faculty dinner. It wasn't to start until seven-thirty—still plenty of time to get him on his cell and ask his opinion on what to do.

His cell rang at least six times before he picked it up. When he did, he was chuckling over something. She could hear others too, laughing in the background.

One other, anyway: it was definitely a woman's giggle.

She was so taken off guard that she stuttered, "Reggie, it's…it's me. Did I, um, catch you at a bad time?"

"Jade? …Oh! No, not at all." From the dead void that followed, she presumed he'd placed his hand over the phone for a moment.

Finally, he said, "There, now I can hear you." There

were only streets sounds now, in the background, so he must have stepped outside. "What's up, Sweetness?"

"Oh…nothing. Who was that?"

"What? Nobody! Nothing at all."

"You were laughing about something." *God, I must sound so needy.*

"It was…nothing really."

"Did I catch you in the middle of something?" *Shit, I sound as if I'm accusing him of something!* "What I mean to say is, did I interrupt a meeting or something?"

"Nah, nothing that can't wait. While I wait for the faculty dinner, I thought I'd take the time to call in a few of the applicants for my teaching assistant position."

"You'll need a teaching assistant?"

"Yes—just a few hours a day. You wouldn't believe how many grad students applied for it. I'm surprised, since the stipend is so low."

"It doesn't matter. Who wouldn't want it on their resumé that they worked with a Nobel Prize winning scholar?" Even Jade was still in awe of that accomplishment. "So, does anyone look interesting?"

"It's going to be a hard decision." Reggie sounded almost gleeful. "But there's one candidate who might be perfect. Sam Hartness. Smart as a whip. Then again, they all are. The thesis on Falstaff clinched it."

Sam Hartness.

Yes! A guy! Yes! "Well, give my hearty congratulations to Sam."

"Will do," Reggie's voice seemed softer. "Now, tell me about your day."

"The Top Moms committee meeting was Machiavellian, to say the least."

He chuckled. "Nothing new there."

"In fact, it's one of the reasons I called. Believe it or not, the committee agreed to all of Lorna's suggestions, including a lottery of all applicants to choose our new members."

"Well, blow me down."

"Yeah, whodathunkit, right? But I was assigned the task of working with Kimberley, of all people, on putting together the lottery—"

Suddenly, another voice could be heard from Reggie's side of the phone. It was a woman's voice, saying something that sounded like, "…Hurry up, Hot Stuff! You're being summoned by the Big Cheese—"

"Reggie," Jade asked, "Are you still there?"

"Gotta go, Sweetness! The faculty reception is about to start. I should be home by nine. Ten, at the latest." His voice sounded distant as he added, "Sam, thanks! Tell them I'll be right there—"

Click.

So, Sam is a woman, Jade realized.

Stunned by this realization, she almost jumped out of her skin as the phone rang again.

He's calling back—good! She tapped open her phone—

"Jade? It's Kimberley."

Oh…heck.

"Jade, please—don't hang up!"

Jade sat there for a moment, until she could tamp down the anger in her voice. "I…wasn't, because I know we've been assigned the coordination of the lottery names." She sighed. "Look, to make it easy on both of us, why don't we just split the list of applicants in half—"

"No need," Kimberley interrupted. "I've already done it. I thought I'd save you the dread of working with me, since you've made it obvious that we're no longer friends."

Jade laughed deliriously. "'No longer?' Be honest, Kimberley: when were we ever friends? You didn't think I'd eventually find out about you and Brady?"

"You have a point," Kimberley conceded. "Then again, with him chasing after Ally, I didn't think you'd take too kindly to hearing about my history with your horny ex-husband."

"*Ally?* Get real! You were fucking him long before she came into the picture. Frankly, I'm happy for her. And, for that matter, I'm happy for Brady too. We should all have what they have: true love and respect for each other."

"How sophisticated. Very French, if I do say so." Kimberley's voice dripped of sarcasm. "You have a point. Why blame Ally for Brady's desertion? I should have blamed the asshole himself—and for that matter, so should you. He researched the club in order to get your little brat a slot. When he learned I was on the Top

Moms committee, he seduced me. I hadn't even met you!"

"True. It was very wrong of Brady to use you. But, admit it, Kimberley: you were ready, willing, and able. You knew Brady was married when you hopped into bed with him."

"He made it clear that he was anything but happy in your so-called marriage," Kimberley retorted. "'So-called' being the operative word here, let me remind you."

"For once, he was right. He'd never be happy with me," Jade admitted. "And I'd never be happy with him." *Only I didn't know it at the time,* Jade thought to herself.

"If that was truly the case, you certainly put on a good act," Kimberley retorted.

Jade sighed. "Is that all you have to say?"

"No. Let me add that he fell in love with Ally, not me, but I'm the one you hate. Go figure."

"Let's not forget that when you discovered that little fact, you did what you could to convince me that she had betrayed me, when in truth she hadn't."

"A mere technicality. We both know it. Otherwise, she wouldn't be with him now." Kimberley paused, then added, "When you barged into my house to confront me about my relationship with Brady, why didn't you believe me?"

"Because I…I found the proof I needed that you were lying to me." *Shut up! Don't mention you have her cell phone!*

"Oh, yeah? What was that?" Kimberley asked suspiciously.

"It was—It was the look on your smug mug," Jade shuddered at the memory. "You're not as good of a liar as you think, Kimberley."

Kimberley was silent. Finally she muttered, "Neither are you, Jade Pierce."

Oh, hell. She knows I stole her phone. As paranoid as she is, she probably thinks I'd mail it to her husband or something.

This bullshit stops here and now. "At least I've moved on," Jade's voice was calm, but firm. "And you should too."

"It's not that easy for some of us." Jade winced at the venom in Kimberley's tone. "Congratulations on snagging your hunky professor. Shakespeare's in love, or something to that effect, eh? And I'm sure he can't believe his luck in landing a kewpie doll sexbot like you. But what are you going to do when your breasts are hanging down to your navel, and you can no longer snake around a pole? You see, eventually men want more than what you can give them, Jade." Kimberley giggled. "I give it a year, tops."

Before Jade could retort, Kimberley hung up.

The sound of the cell phone hitting the wall woke Oliver.

"Poopy!" he yelled. "Mama! Poo-*PEE*!"

She wiped her tears and set her lips into a placid smile before starting down the hall toward the nursery.

7:11 p.m.

"I'M SO SORRY! AM I DISTURBING YOUR DINNER?" It surprised Kimberley that Bettina and Eleanor allowed Lily to answer the door of the Morrow-Connaught residence.

Then again, Bettina's mutt, Prince Vsevolod, was at her feet.

The dog's growl was silenced with a hand motion from the little girl. Lily shrugged. "You will, if you hang around." She stared closely at Kimberley. "Mummy is indisposed."

"Yes, I see." Kimberley craned her neck in order to scope out her prey beyond the vast foyer. Ah, there was Bettina, with her mother, Eleanor, anxiously pacing the thick wool carpet in the large, sumptuous living room beyond.

A few snippets of their tense conversation wafted her way. She caught the phrases, "—Heights Country Day School" and "—ruined Lily's future."

Oh, to be a fly on one of those walls, Kimberley thought.

Noting the smirk on Kimberley's face, Lily did the only thing she could to block the woman's view: she stepped outside, closing the door behind her. "You're one of my mother's Top Moms, aren't you?"

"Yes! I'm Mrs. Savitch." She held out her hand.

Lily stared down at it, but didn't take it.

Kimberley dropped her arm by her side. "You're being rude. I wonder what your mother would think of your behavior."

"She would probably laugh. She knows you don't like her."

"Really? She knows? ...I mean, is that what she thinks?" It slipped out before Kimberley realized she said it out loud.

Lily said, "My mother may be mean, but she's not stupid."

Out of the mouths of babes.

Suddenly, the door swung open. Bettina looked out. "Lily, what are you doing out here? Even Pacific Heights has a homeless vagrant or two" —She scowled when she realized Kimberley was there as well—"or three. Kimberley, to what do we owe the honor?"

Kimberley nodded toward Lily. "May we speak in private?"

Bettina thought for a moment. Finally, she nodded at Lily.

The little girl stepped inside, slamming the door behind her.

Kimberley faked a smile. "Precocious, isn't she?"

"You aren't here to chide me regarding my daughter. Knowing Lily, if she insulted you somehow, more than likely you deserved it. So, get to the point."

Kimberley's grin faded. "I...I wish to apologize to you."

Bettina arched a brow. "Oh? Why, pray tell?"

"For my lack of enthusiasm toward Lorna's suggestions." She hesitated. "But, to be perfectly honest, I was getting mixed signals from you."

Bettina acknowledged her declaration with a shrug. "Perhaps."

"As far as the club is concerned, you've always been its standard bearer. To see you usurped in that role..." She let her thought peter out.

Not to worry. By the way in which Bettina winced, Kimberley knew she'd gotten her message across.

"Especially when it comes to whom the club lets through its prestigious doors," she continued. "Oh, don't get me wrong! I understand her desire that the process be a bit more broadminded. And, yet, it would be disconcerting to see a mass exodus of current club members, just because she wishes to carry out some sort of inane, ill-conceived social experiment."

"I see your point," Bettina nodded grudgingly. "But we took a vote, and it stands."

"Don't get me wrong, Bettina. I totally agree with you that a lottery should take place." She sighed longingly. "It's just *so* disappointing! Like the rest of us, I'm sure you had your 'dream team' of mothers already chosen. Wouldn't it be grand if even some of them won the lottery?"

Suddenly, Bettina's eyes opened wide.

That's when Kimberley knew she understood the scheme.

To assure they were on the same page, Kimberley added, "And, as our founder, I presume it'll be your role to choose the *winning names*."

"I've no doubt some of them will be chosen—perhaps even by me," Bettina purred. "Karma, and all that. You're quite a little trooper—a real team player, and I appreciate it. Tell me: considering the unfortunate incident that tore asunder our previously idyllic allegiance—"

"You mean, the fact that I'm practically destitute, thanks to the connivances of that oafish bore you married?"

"You have such a delicate way with words, Kimberley. But, yes, I'll grant you that: Art did screw you over. Trust me, I got it in the end too—"

It was on the tip of Kimberley's tongue to retort, *Yeah, I know. I saw the pictures—Andy's that is*, but she kept her mouth shut rather than defeat the real purpose of the call:

Ruining Bettina's life, once and for all.

"—metaphorically speaking, so I feel your pain," Bettina continued. "So, why the sudden change of heart?"

"It's simple. We both need a public forum in which to show the world we're still alive and kicking—better yet, thriving, and doing good deeds for others. As long as we control the club, it affords us that."

"We're just two votes," Bettina reminded her.

"Mallory is game."

"No surprise there," Bettina sneered. "Anything that allows her to lord it over others is catnip to her."

"And Sally is malleable," Kimberley added.

"True that." Bettina hesitated. "The current bylaws call for one instance in which a vote by all but one will be necessary for the removal of PHM&T's CEM."

Kimberley frowned. "But...but that person is you." *Oh, brother! Is this yet another one of Bettina's loyalty tests?*

"Correct. But you forget. As of this morning, Lorna shares the position with me."

Kimberley pursed her lips. "There is no way that Jade will vote against her."

"Why is that?" Bettina's gaze dared her to glance away. "What happened between you and Jade? You two used to be thick as thieves."

"Nothing! A...a simple misunderstanding." She frowned. She hardly wanted to let Bettina in on the real reason that Jade never even attempted to call her back, all this time.

Wait—it happened right around the time my phone went missing...

Oh my God. Jade has it. And she's seen Andy's photos.
Why, that bitch...

"If it's a mere kerfuffle, then it should be easy for you to kiss and make up," Bettina proclaimed. "Because we'll need her vote, too, when the time comes. In the meantime, I'll text you the list of preferred candidates, so that you can prepare the Post-Its tonight." She counted down on her fingers. "Since we've opened it up to twenty members per age group, I'll be drawing all twenty Onesies, and at least ten of the rest of the groups of Twosies, Threesies, Foursies, and after-kindergarten Fivesies, as well as replacements for those misguided member defections." She thought for a moment, and then added, "For the sake of appearances, I presume I should let Lorna draw a few."

"If you say so." The thought that Kelly had a fifty-fifty chance of being drawn by the two women who hated her most brought Kimberley out of her trance.

Kelly would certainly get a kick out of it too.

Come to think of it, better Kelly should learn about Bettina and Andy via the pictures than through Kimberley.

As far as she was concerned, she'd sit back and enjoy the fireworks.

I've got to get that cell phone from Jade—and the sooner, the better.

CHAPTER SEVEN

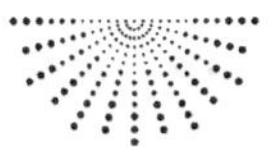

Wednesday, 4 September
6:45 a.m.

BETTINA HADN'T SLEPT WELL IN HER NEW QUARTERS. Obviously the same plush mattresses used upstairs in the Morrow-Connaught mansion weren't considered necessary in the former servants' quarters. To top it off, Bettina was sure the sheets weren't one hundred percent cotton, either, because she woke up scratching.

Oh my God, she thought, what if I've been infected with bed bugs?!

She leaped out of bed so furiously that she roused Prince Vsevolod from his deep slumber. He opened one eye, glared at her, and then rolled to the other side of the pillow that served as his new floor mat.

I hope he pees on it, Bettina thought. It would serve

Eleanor right, taking my word that I'd prefer to be in this dungeon.

Had Bettina been sleeping in her own bed right now on the twenty-fifth floor of the Summit, the sun would have awakened her as it rose over Mount Diablo's twin peaks in the East Bay. By now, the sun's rays would have already spread over the calm waters of San Francisco Bay, where tiny white sailboats dodged and darted between the cargo ships coming into port. From such a lofty height, all of it looked like a child's miniature toy set come to life.

It was all a fantasy, Bettina thought. *And now, this is my reality. My home and belongings will be auctioned off to the highest bidder. My daughter has been exiled from the school that my family nurtured to its current state of academic supremacy.*

And my own sister-in-law is trying to rob me of the club I founded.

What blasphemy!

She took solace in the fact that Kimberley had come around to realizing where her loyalties lay. Soon, she'd be able to put Lorna in her place. And for that matter, Eleanor too, for being so presumptuous as to assume she needed help bringing the club back to its renowned status.

She walked quietly out of the room, so as not to wake Lily, who slept in the small trundle bed beside the dresser. She couldn't bear watching her sob through the day.

Even if the Cross name was now mud, surely one of the other private elementary schools wouldn't mind being associated with the Connaught name, and the largesse that went with it. The moment she got home from the lottery, she'd begin calling around.

7:05 a.m.

LORNA AWOKE, ONLY TO DISCOVER THAT MATTHEW HAD never come to bed.

This, despite finally answering her numerous and increasingly anxious calls and texts with a text of his own, assuring her that, *"Dante and I are fine! Ran into an old college buddy while we were jogging. Catching up on old times. We'll be home by midnight."*

She fell asleep around two in the morning, with still no husband or son.

She ran into Dante's room. She was relieved to see that her son was in his crib, sound asleep. At least they'd come home sometime during the night.

And yet, Matthew had headed out again, early this morning. Where? And for that matter, why?

Gently, she kissed her son's cheek.

Before she showered, she tried Matthew's cell phone.

It rolled over to voice mail. She hoped her tone made it quite clear what she expected of him. "I have a meeting at nine today. I hope you'll be home at least by eight forty-five, to watch Dante for me. Also, I have a doctor's appointment at twelve forty-five. I presume you'll want to be there for it too."

By eight-forty, when Matthew hadn't shown up, she called the one person she thought might actually know something about his whereabouts: Eleanor.

Her mother-in-law was dumbfounded by her question. "I swear, Lorna, he's kept me in the dark as well!" She paused, then added, "Why is it that I'm only hearing about his mysterious comings and goings now?"

"What with Art's disappearance, and Bettina's legal battles, I felt you had enough on your plate," Lorna explained.

"Someday, I hope your daughter-in-law doesn't make a similar decision on your behalf," she retorted dryly.

Considering Dante's autism, the hope that he might someday have a loving, caring wife was a bittersweet fantasy of Lorna's. She sighed. "Of course, you're right, Eleanor. Please, forgive me."

"No, I should ask your forgiveness. It was a stupid thing to say." Obviously, the sadness in her daughter-in-law's voice prompted Eleanor to lighten up.

"I'm just…well, I guess this pregnancy has me jumpy. Something just doesn't feel right." There. Lorna said what she was feeling out loud for the first time.

"You should see your doctor immediately." The now obvious concern in Eleanor's voice was comforting to Lorna.

"I have an appointment this afternoon, in fact. Twelve forty-five."

"Would you…well, would you mind if I came along?"

"Really, it's not necessary."

"Perhaps not for you, Lorna, but I'd like to feel needed by another woman whom I love and respect. You are as close to me as my own daughter, but right now, she feels the need to push me away." Eleanor's voice was racked with hurt.

"In fact, I'd appreciate the company," Lorna admitted.

Ideally, Matthew's. But since he was just as inconsiderate as his sister, she'd take what she could get, even if it happened to be her mother-in-law.

Lorna hesitated, then added, "Do me a favor and don't mention to Hera that you'll be joining me. She'll want to come along as well, and frankly, I'd rather not turn this into a free for all."

"No need to worry," Eleanor promised. "Hera is down in Half Moon Bay. Something about a beach ceremony, then a harvest celebration."

Thank goodness, Lorna thought. "And, one more thing: would you mind if I dropped Dante with you this morning? Today is the Top Moms Committee's lottery for new members."

"Then I presume Bettina will be there as well."

"Yes, of course."

"Good! When you drop Dante here, you can pick her up and take her with you."

"Oh! …Sure, of course. But, wouldn't she be coming from Lily's school drop-off?"

"In light of Art's dealings, Lily was denied her slot at Pacific Heights Country Day School."

"I'm sorry to hear that. I'm sure Bettina is quite upset."

"She's loaded for bear. She's not the only one. I'm in the process of twisting a few arms right now, but it may come down to yet another lawsuit." She sighed. "I'll see you and our little man in a few minutes."

Bettina is on the warpath again. Great, just what I need. I'll be fighting for every name that doesn't pass Bettina's sniff test. Well, at least Jade will have my back.

If only Ally and Jillian could be there with them too.

8:37 a.m.

Bright and early, with Oliver in hand, Jade rang the bell at Brady's house.

Ally opened the door, Zoe on her hip.

Jade held Oliver out to her. "It's lottery day. I'm off to do battle with Bettina."

"Wow! She agreed to Lorna's terms?" Ally blinked, both to get the sleep out of her eyes, and because she couldn't believe her ears. "You mean, she agreed to it?"

Jade nodded. "Along with Lorna's other terms,

including single moms and working moms—both terms that, if I remember correctly, you fall under."

"Lucky me," Ally retorted. "Still, I'll pass on the honor of reapplying."

"But—"

"And quid pro quo on babysitting. We'll be dropping the kids with you tomorrow, because we have a meeting with a new supplier for Happy Feet. Oliver, wave bye-bye to Mommy!"

Before Jade could protest—about Ally's club membership, let alone the babysitting on the only day Reggie had off all week—she closed the door firmly.

She'll change her mind the moment Lorna and I tell her she was one of the lottery winners, Jade reasoned.

Oh, heck! I forgot to make up a Post-It with her name!

The stationery store on Chestnut Street wouldn't be open until ten o'clock. Still, she had just enough time to pick up the Post-Its at the Walgreens.

Since she didn't know what color Kimberley used for the lottery, she bought one packet of each, cramming them into her purse.

Outside the library, Jade dumped all the Post-It packets onto the passenger seat. Carefully, she wrote Ally's name on one slip from each packet. After folding the slips in half, she slipped them into her purse.

She entered the library's community room in time to see Kimberley shake the Post-It slips into a clear bowl.

The slips were yellow.

She pocketed the yellow slip with Ally's name. When Lorna arrived, she'd palm it to her right before they chose the three replacements for the new Twosies group.

8:51 a.m.

"Bettina, your ride is here," Eleanor called down the back stairwell.

Bettina shrugged. *I guess Mother needs her car today,* she reasoned. *It was the only reason why Eleanor would have texted for an Uber limo.*

She took one look at herself in the small bathroom mirror. She was pleased with the picture she presented in her Akris Punto matchstick print shift, which was loose enough to hide the slightest of baby bumps. But she could only imagine what flaws might appear in her make-up once she got out of the horrid servants' quarters bathroom and into the light of day.

No matter. Her Uber profile forbade the drivers to talk to her, much less look at her.

Thank goodness they don't rate passengers the way we rate them, she thought. *It would add insult to injury, since as it is, they never seem to be around when I need them.*

She entered the foyer to find Eleanor holding Dante. Lorna stood at her side.

Oh no.

"Ready?" her sister-in-law asked. Lorna's lips were forced into a smile. "Matthew had a meeting, so Eleanor offered to sit for Dante."

"It will be wonderful, having both my grandchildren to entertain me this morning," Eleanor's look dared Bettina to balk at her decision.

"Thanks for the offer, but it's such a beautiful morning. I think I'll walk to the library," Bettina retorted coolly.

"Straight down Steiner—and in those shoes?" Eleanor's eyes dropped to Bettina's four-inch banjo spiked cap-toe Louboutin booties. "If you don't crack a heel, you might break an ankle. With what you've got in the bank, neither is replaceable."

Bettina glared crossly at her mother.

"Oops, got to go, or we'll be late," Lorna took Bettina's hand and nudged her out the door.

Bettina got into the passenger seat, then slammed the car door. "Don't expect a tip," she warned Lorna.

"I won't, but I have one for you: be kinder to Eleanor. She loves you, but she needs you to show her that her love is appreciated."

"Who the hell are you to give me a lecture?" Bettina growled. "No, don't answer that. I'm sure you feel that marrying into the Connaught name and money has earned you the right. Well, it hasn't. And as much as you'd like to usurp me as a Connaught, you never will. Eventually, my mother will see right through you. When she does, I will take full advantage of your fall from grace."

"I wouldn't doubt it in the least," Lorna said sadly.

She started the car.

They made the eight-block ride in silence.

9:02 a.m.

"WELL, WELL, ISN'T THAT COZY! BETTINA RODE OVER WITH Lorna," Mallory snarled.

"Why is that so bad? They live just a few blocks from each other," Sally pointed out.

"No, not any more," Kimberley replied. "Since the Feds raided her place, Bettina's been camping out at her mother's house." Still, it surprised her too, in light of her newfound allegiance with Bettina. At least, she hoped Bettina was still under the assumption that Kimberley was on her side.

The look of sheer hate on Bettina's face gave her the answer she sought.

Good, now for some real fun, Kimberley thought. She waved at Lorna and Bettina. "Ladies, welcome! Shall we get started?"

10: 22 a.m.

"—AND THE SEVENTEENTH ONESIES SLOT GOES TO"—Bettina put her hand into the bowl, only to withdraw it, clasping yet another folded Post-It slip. Peeling back the slip, she read—"Julie Unger."

"Ha! The wife of that commercial realtor who gives all the money to the symphony?" Mallory nodded grudgingly. "Well, I guess this lottery idea hasn't been such a disaster after all."

Lorna pursed her lips. She took the opposite opinion of the names drawn thus far, all were the well-heeled wives of San Francisco up-and-comers, or movers-and-shakers.

Mallory is right, though, Lorna thought. It was my idea, and it's been a fair drawing, and both Jade and Kimberley put the names in the bowl, so there's nothing I can say.

Almost as if reading her mind, Bettina declared, "My arm is tired from lifting all these heavyweights into the club. Lorna, my darling co-Chief Executive Mom, why don't you take a turn at it?"

Smiling sweetly, she handed the bowl to Lorna.

None of the last three Onesies moms were any different from the other seventeen: all rising stars in San Francisco's social firmament.

The fix had to be in—but how?

"Why don't we take a break, so that Kimberley can set up the lottery for the Twosies? Remember, ladies, there are three slots available, and we have twenty-four applicants."

With a grin, Kimberley took the bowl from Lorna. "This will only take a moment," she promised.

Lorna shook her head. She headed outside for some fresh air.

Jade must have had the same idea. She'd already plopped down on a bench in the library's courtyard.

Lorna did the same. "How is this happening? Bettina's mommy group wet dream is coming true in front of our eyes."

"It's my fault. I allowed Kimberley to talk me into letting her prepare the lottery by herself."

"But…why would you do that?"

"Because I can't stand the thought of being near her! Not after learning about her affair with Brady."

Lorna turned to stare at her. "What? Why am I just hearing about this now?"

"It happened before he asked me to come home, and before he fell in love with Ally. When he realized she was the one who had poisoned me against Ally, he came clean about it. I confronted Kimberley. She denied it, of course. But then I…I found evidence that she lied."

"And now, she's in cahoots with Bettina in getting the club back to the way it was. I'm going to call their bluff on it, right now!" Lorna rose angrily.

Jade pulled her back down onto the bench. "Wait! We're doing this for Eleanor, right?"

Lorna nodded.

"Eleanor wants Bettina to clear her name. If all these new snooty-hooty mothers can see Bettina being a good mom and a good social leader, it accomplishes that goal, right?"

"I...I guess so." Lorna shook her head. "It's just not right! We'll always be outnumbered."

"There's still Ally." Jade put her hand into Lorna's.

Lorna felt something.

"Don't look down at your hand. Palm it until it's time to choose a Twosies family."

"Jade!! Did you—"

"I sure as hell did!" Jade grinned mischievously. "Think of the look on Bettina's face when you say her name."

That was enough to convince Lorna.

She laughed, then sauntered inside.

10:34 p.m.

"*ALLY THORNTON?*" THE FACT THAT KIMBERLEY AND Bettina practically shouted that out at the same time as Lorna called her name was all the proof Lorna needed that they'd fixed the lottery.

"Wait...I don't remember Ally's re-submission," Kimberley stuttered.

"It came in before midnight, last night," Jade assured

her. "So, of course, it qualifies."

"But, of course," Bettina muttered. "Still, since she was found lacking as a member in the past, I don't see how we can accept her again."

"Our rules have changed," Lorna countered. "We now accept both single and working mothers. As far as her abilities to carry out tasks, prior to your finding out about those issues, you and the rest of the Top Moms Committee rated her admirably." Lorna held out the bowl to Bettina. "Perhaps you'd like to choose the rest of the families for the Twosies slots."

Bettina practically tore the bowl out of Lorna's hand. "Thank you, yes, I'll take things from here." She reached into the bowl, but then did a double-take.

"Who is it?" Mallory asked.

"It's...*Kelly Overton*." Bettina glared at Lorna.

Lorna's eyes opened wide. Her shock was evident in her gasp, and the peals of laughter that followed.

As far as Bettina was concerned, Jade's snickers were no less egregious.

However, it did prove that neither of them had anything to do with Kelly's inclusion—unless they were that good at faking it. In Jade's case, she'd believe it, considering her former profession.

Laughter isn't always acceptable at Top Moms meetings, let alone this contagious. Sally couldn't help but giggle along. Finally, she gasped, "Why are we all laughing?"

"We are not 'all' laughing," Bettina snapped. Her glare zeroed in on Lorna. "Can you explain how yet another former member's application was included—let alone one who cheated at her probationary membership task? In fact, why, and when, was she allowed to reapply?"

Lorna's smile faded. "As always, your accusation is baseless. I'm not the one who prepared the lottery slips, remember?"

Bettina turned her glare toward Kimberley.

Kimberley met it head-on, with absolute innocence. "Like Ally's application, Kelly's also came in late last night. Look, we all know she cheated by getting Stanlee Gatti to do her table settings at last year's Thanksgiving potluck, but is that worse than getting hit with a lawsuit for defamation of character?"

"What the hell are you talking about?" Bettina sputtered. "We never threw a lawsuit at her!"

"You've got it backwards. Kelly is threatening to take *us* to court, for defaming *her*. She feels she'll win easily, considering what has come to light regarding you, our fearless founder. She may be right. Her offense looks like child's play in comparison."

Bettina arched a brow. "Pray tell, what exactly was I supposed to have done?"

"Aid and abet your husband by recruiting clients for him from the club's members."

Bettina turned and glared at Jade, who shook her head as a plea of innocence.

"Kelly claims you put the screws to her, for one," Kimberley continued. "That being said, I felt that accepting her application was the lesser of two evils. And, now that she's actually been chosen, it's another win for the club, wouldn't you say?"

No one dared to argue, least of all Bettina.

"We still have to replace one more Twosies defection, as well as another ten new members," Lorna pointed out. "Shall we continue the drawing?"

She was not at all surprised that Bettina's wish list continued being drawn without further surprises. No matter. The wariness in Bettina's eyes was worth it.

No surprise: Bettina adjourned the meeting immediately after the drawing.

CHAPTER EIGHT

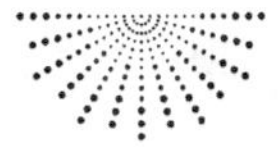

12:24 p.m.

On the way back to Eleanor's house, neither Lorna nor Bettina said a word to the other. Later, Lorna would liken it to an exchange of political prisoners through Korea's Demilitarized Zone:

She pulled up to Eleanor's house.

Bettina got out of the car, walking quickly toward the house.

Eleanor walked out of the house, holding Dante.

As the two women passed each other, Eleanor handed Dante to Bettina. "While you're calling schools, you can spend a little time with your nephew until Matthew gets back. Supposedly, he's on his way."

"But…" Bettina's protest was stopped by the look in her mother's eye. Furiously, she walked into the house.

"That went well," Eleanor said cheerfully.

All Lorna could think of was that Matt still hadn't answered her calls, and he was still not home.

Where the hell was he?

1:05 p.m.

"Yes, well…but of course, I certainly understand your 'concern' for your school's reputation." Bettina rolled her eyes. She'd heard this same argument from the last six head-of-schools on her list. "At the same time, I am somewhat disappointed that you feel you have to judge my daughter by her father's actions as opposed to her own merits, particularly in light of the fact that, within your admissions literature, you make such a point about seeking out and nurturing, and I quote, 'the exceptional child with whom compromise is never an option, and whose future should never be compromised'."

Whatever the fuck *that* particular hooey means, she thought.

In any event, it sounded haughty enough, she reasoned. And it certainly beat placement in a public school.

Time to turn on the charm. "If any child's future is being compromised, it is certainly Lily's! And through no fault of her own," Bettina continued. "She is a Connaught, through and through. Her grandmother, Eleanor, is known for her patronage of several charities. She is also the benefactress of numerous cultural organizations, not to mention some of the city's most noted academic institutions...Me? Well, besides my patronage of both the opera and the ballet, I am the founder of the Pacific Heights Moms & Tots Club...yes, it *is quite* popular, isn't it? ...You applied once, yourself, you say? ...As a working mother, *and* a Size Ten? *Hmmm*...In the interim, we've worked diligently on rectifying the issue of, as you so creatively put it, our lack of diversity...Oh, *really*? Tit for tat: your own issues with diversity might be alleviated by allowing the child of a fugitive safe harbor within the walls of your estab—"

Click.

"Hello? Are you still there?"

The dial tone indicated otherwise.

Lily looked up from the floor, where she played with Dante. "Mummy, did that school say no too?"

"Yes," Bettina admitted, "But only because it has no more slots."

For the children of con men on the lam, anyway.

With trembling hands, Bettina punched in the number of the San Francisco Unified School District.

"Hello, I'd like to enroll my child into kindergarten... Yes, I know that school started yesterday. My bad...Where do I live? Russian Hill. Oops, I mean Pacific Heights...*No,*

I didn't mean to *mislead* you in order to get my child into a better school! …Yes, I'm in front of my computer. Let me look up my child's designated 'attendance area school,' as you suggest."

Bettina logged onto the school district's website, then onto the address look-up tool, in order to find the school assigned to Eleanor's address.

Not so good. The way the school's boundaries were drawn, even students who lived in Pacific Heights were relegated to Lincoln Elementary, in the Tenderloin, one of the poorer sections of the city. Scanning the school's grade statistics, she noted that its students were at least twenty percent below the district's grade averages across all subjects.

Oh, my God, she realized, this is a ghetto school!

"Since we're on the topic, are certain schools better than others? …What does that mean, 'slots in the schools are given out by tentative assignment'? …Ah, I see, computer-generated assignments, depending on your top ten schools." Bettina was pulling up the various schools' test scores when the woman said something that stopped her cold. "*What?* Tentative assignment has *already* taken place? So, where does that leave my child?"

"As I mentioned, your assigned school is Lincoln Elementary—" The woman's voice was bored, her words firm.

"I'm sorry, but the assignation is inappropriate for my child. You see, her bloodline is both Connaught *and*

Morrow…*Excuse me*! *ARE YOU LAUGHING AT ME?*" Bettina held the phone away from her ear.

When she could stand it no longer, she hung up.

She walked out onto the terrace, so that Lily couldn't see her crying.

A few minutes later, after she'd composed herself, Lily felt sorry enough for her to come outside too. She was holding Dante's hand in order to help him toddle toward his aunt.

Bettina scooped him into her arms. She held him up so that they were nose to nose. His eyes gazed away from hers.

For the first time, she noticed they were the same shade of green as her father's eyes.

How she wished her father were alive now, to give her guidance.

No, really, she needed a man to kick ass for her.

My God, I'm so tired of doing it all on my own.

Had she not been cradling Dante, the poop in his diaper would have missed the sleeve of her dress—

Oh…*hell.*

Sniffing the air, Prince Vsevolod backed away from her. Not that she could blame him.

The front door's chime could not have been more poorly timed.

Who the hell could it be?

She walked to the front door and peeked through the keyhole:

Matthew. He waved at her, then gave her the high sign.

She swung open the door. "It's about damn time—"

Seeing that he wasn't alone, she stopped mid-sentence.

Daniel Warwick was standing beside him. Apparently she'd interrupted them because they were laughing about something.

She was sure it had something to do with her. "Oh! Mr. Warwick. What are you doing here?"

"Did you forget that we have a lunch date?"

"No! …I mean…I'm so sorry—"

Matthew's nose went in the air. "What's that smell?"

Suddenly, she remembered that she reeked of baby poo. She handed Dante to his father, but backed off instead of taking the hand Daniel offered. "I should, er, change first."

She stumbled out of the foyer.

She tripped on the third step of the stairwell down to the servants' quarters as she heard Matthew ask Lily, "Why are you guys sleeping down there?"

"Because Mummy is punishing Grandma Connaught. But I don't mind. I'm pretending I'm Cinderella, and that Mummy is the wicked stepmother."

"Wow, Lily," Matthew was awed. "That's…*harsh*—"

Bettina slammed the door.

So, that's how my daughter views me? she wondered. I'm the villainess in her fairytale life?

Maybe the ghetto school will teach her a lesson as to how good she really has it, even with me as her mother.

She quickly shed the Akris Punto shift for a long-sleeved wool crepe Saint Laurent leopard print dress with a bateau neckline. She picked up the stained dress. She stopped herself from dropping it into the trash. Heaven knows, she'd never wear it again, but perhaps she could sell it on consignment.

Of course, the cost of dry cleaning will probably be half the cost of the dress, she reasoned. Maybe I should soak it first? If it comes out that way, I'll save a few bucks...

Only after the dress was submerged in the sink did she think to look at the dress's maintenance tag: DRY CLEAN ONLY.

She took the sopping wet dress from the sink, and threw it into the trash.

This being poor crap sucks, she thought.

When she felt presentable, she walked upstairs. Matthew must have been changing Dante, because Lily was alone with Daniel. They sat on the floor. Daniel stroked Prince Vsevolod's belly, while Lily was using colored markers on a white pad.

Lily held up her painting. "Guess what I painted, Mummy!"

To Bettina's eye, it looked like a four-legged blob. Her smile wavered. "Why, that's easy. It's Prince Vsevolod."

"Wrong," Lily declared adamantly. "It's a *horse*."

Bettina's eyes grew big.

At that moment, she realized that Daniel was watching her. "You've got quite a little artist here."

"Yes, well, all children enjoy colors and textures. Lily is no exception there." Bettina's laugh was tepid at best.

"Oh, I wouldn't say that. Her horse sculpture is pretty spectacular."

Lily looked up. "My…what?"

"You remember, honey," Bettina shook her head slightly and prayed that Lily could hear the desperation in her voice. "The one in our former dining room—in the penthouse we no longer own, th*anks to Mr. Warwick here.*"

Lily frowned. She was about to say something when Matthew shouted, "Lily, quick! I need Dante's diaper bag."

She grabbed it and ran down the hall.

Bettina nudged Daniel toward the front door. "Shall we go?"

"Just when things were getting interesting," he murmured.

Also 1:05 p.m.

"DO YOU WANT TO SEE YOUR DAUGHTER?" DR. MORTENSEN asked.

"It's…a girl?" Lorna and Eleanor exclaimed in unison.

The doctor turned back to the ultrasound image—and

did a double-take. He tilted his head, and then laughed. "Sorry, I'm wrong. You're having a son, *and* a daughter."

"*Twins*?" Eleanor and Lorna squealed at the same time.

"Looks like it." Dr. Mortensen turned the monitor so that they could see it.

Both women leaned in. Eleanor clasped Lorna's hand. "I wish Matthew were here," she whispered.

Lorna turned away, but not before the doctor saw the sadness in her face.

She was glad when he launched into the extra care instructions he felt she'd need, now that she was carrying two instead of one. For once, she was glad Eleanor was there, if only to listen for her, since all Lorna could think about was what she'd say to Matthew when he finally surfaced.

2:08 p.m.

"You haven't touched your salad," Daniel chided Bettina. "For that matter, you haven't said a word since we ordered."

"I—I guess I'm mesmerized by the view," she sighed.

He'd taken her outside of the city—across the Golden Gate Bridge, to Marin County. In fact, they were in the bayside town of Tiburon. It was late enough in the day that even the usual smattering of tourist patrons had dispersed by now. Far off in the distance beyond Alcatraz and Angel Islands, the skyline of the city could easily be seen from where they were sitting, on the deck of Sam's Anchor Café.

It seems so far away, Bettina thought.

If only her troubles felt that way as well.

The biggest of which was sitting right next to her, chowing down on a grilled rib-eye steak.

Let the inquisition begin. "Why are we here, Mr. Warwick?"

Daniel's smile disappeared. He patted his mouth with his napkin, then took a sip of his wine. "Bettina, I know my investigation has put you in a tenuous position, to say the least—"

"The *very* least," she muttered.

"Let's not forget the crab salad you just got out of it." Daniel smiled. "But that doesn't have to be the only thing that comes your way—that is, if you play ball."

"Oh? And just what would that entail?" Now that he was finally getting down to brass tacks, Bettina lost what little appetite she had.

"To put it bluntly, Bettina, now is the time for you to cozy up to me." He leaned in toward her. "The sooner you give up the goods, the better."

A chill of excitement climbed up Bettina's spine. *He's propositioning me.*

Finally, her eyes met his. "And if I, as you so exquisitely put it, 'give up the goods,' what will I get in return?"

He arched a brow. "What would you like?"

"Ideally, I'd like my life back—sans that conniving douchebag of a husband, of course. I want my home. I want my furnishings. I want access to my bank accounts as well as my trust fund." She laid her hand over his. "Is that too much for a girl to ask?"

"It depends on what you're willing to give up in return." His naughty grin made her heart beat all the faster.

"Name it," she murmured.

He flipped her hand over, so that it was palm-up. Then, very slowly, he traced her lifeline. "I think I've made myself perfectly clear. So, when do you want to give it up?"

"The sooner the better, if it gets me all I want."

He laughed. "That's my girl! By the way, there's a reward in it—that is, if you go all the way."

Go all the way.

It was on the tip of her tongue to ask if he meant her to be the sub, but why bother, she thought. She'd seen the way his eyes grew when he saw all of her paddles, and the smirk that followed. To get her old life back, she'd just have to take her lumps, and not just figuratively speaking.

The thought made her wince, bringing to mind the odious experience she'd had with Andy Hepburn.

It reminded her that, for all she knew, she was carrying Andy's baby. She didn't know which was worse, if it were Andy's, or Art's. The only consolation was that, with both of them out of her life, the child would be all hers.

Like Lily, would her baby eventually end up hating her?

If she could get their old life back—so that the infant would always be provided for, and so that Lily could forgive her—it was worth making a pact with this new devil.

She nodded. "Sure, I'm in."

He winked. "It'll be worth your while." He threw down the bills needed to cover their meal. "I guess we should get to it."

Her eyes opened wide. "Wait…you mean, today? Like, *right now*?"

He shook his head. "I told you, the decision is yours to make. There can be no coercion on my part. Your attorneys would throw that into the mix, and the deal would be null and void."

"No, no—of course it's my decision. And I wouldn't breathe a word of it to my attorneys." She took a deep breath. "I'd like to wait until Saturday, if you don't mind."

"By all means."

"Tell me then: when? And where?"

"I think we'd be more comfortable at my hotel: the Fairmont, on Nob Hill. Let's say one o'clock." He chuckled. "You can practically walk to the Summit from there—that is, if you've earned back the keys."

When you get through with me, I doubt I'll feel like

walking to the bed, much less down one hill, and up the other, she thought.

She knew he was watching her as she walked to the door.

She never felt so low—all the more reason to hold her head high.

2:15 p.m.

"Twins," Matthew whispered the word.

He looks just as stunned as I felt when I heard the news, Lorna realized.

"I...I don't know what to say," he stuttered.

"You can start by telling your wife how much you love her," Eleanor suggested dryly.

"But, of course I do." Matthew bent to kiss Lorna.

When his lips brushed her forehead, she felt as if it were on fire.

"A gesture was worth a thousand words, but I don't think that's the case," Eleanor warned him.

"We should be going," Lorna took Dante from Matthew. "Will you be following us home in your car?" she asked him.

"Of course," he said sharply. "Where else would I be going?"

"Good question," she muttered.

She didn't wait for his reply. Instead, she walked out the door.

2:30 p.m.

APPARENTLY, DANTE HADN'T TAKEN A NAP WITH EITHER Bettina or Matthew watching him because he fell asleep the moment she laid him on his crib mattress.

As she watched her son's chest rise and fall in slumber, Matthew's hand went around her waist.

"Why didn't you answer my calls and texts?" She asked the question without turning around.

"Because I couldn't." The sentence was nuzzled into her ear.

"Yes, you could have, if that was what you'd wanted." She turned around to face him. "Matthew, please tell me what is happening! Where do you go, and with whom?"

He took both her hands in his. "Lorna, please, just this once: trust me that what I'm doing now is for the health and wellbeing of our family. In a few months' time, I'll be able to tell you everything."

"A few months? No, Matthew! I can't deal with this now—not with all that is happening with Bettina, and with carrying a child...*two* children!"

"But, I can't! All I can say is..." His eyes scanned the room, as if seeking the words he needed to convince her. Finally, they tumbled out. "Lorna, Dante's autism was a real wake-up call to me. Had he been 'perfect'—I hate that word because no one is perfect. Still, you know what I mean—"

"No! In all honesty, I don't. Please, explain yourself."

"Had he been well, I would still be going through a...a *benign* life."

She shook her head, confused. "No, sorry, I really don't know what you mean."

"By that, I mean a life in which I barely feel anything beyond the pleasantness created by our wealth. I'd have nothing to offer, because I would not have been challenged."

"All parents with special needs children are challenged. What makes us any different from anyone else?"

"We have money. We have influence. If we can't use it to change the world—to change our child's world—then why us?"

Why us, indeed.

Is this why God gave us Dante?

She placed her hands on Matthew's face, to pull him down into her kiss.

When their lips parted, she sighed. "I won't ask again, and I'll give you between now, and when the twins are born. *But that's it.*"

"It's all the time I need," he assured her.

Then he kissed her again—

Only, this time, he did not let her go.

She was fine with that.

His kiss lasted beyond the threshold of Dante's room.

By the time they fell into their bed, he had undressed her.

She waited until he was on his back before stripping him of his shirt and his pants, and anything else that kept them from having make-up sex.

Afterward, she realized she'd given him a reprieve.

This was okay with her, if only, succeed or fail, he would have followed his heart.

Now, with her blessing.

CHAPTER NINE

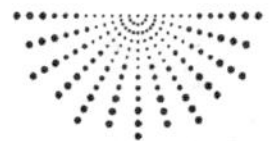

Thursday, 5 September
8:15 a.m.

LILY WAS LATE ON HER FIRST DAY AT LINCOLN ELEMENTARY because Bettina had a hell of a time finding parking for Eleanor's car that was anywhere near the school's Tenderloin location, off Polk Street. To top it off, three panhandlers accosted them in the short distance between her parking space and the school, including one woman with a baby on her arm and a little girl clinging to her leg.

"Mummy, shouldn't we give the woman with the two children some money?"

"I would, but I don't have any small bills on me." In truth, Bettina abhorred beggars. Besides, she needed to hold onto what little money she had: two ten-dollar bills, and some loose change.

Suddenly, the thought struck her: *My God, this woman could be me in another year or two.*

Quickly, she shuttled Lily down the block and into the schoolyard.

The differences between Lincoln Elementary and Pacific Heights Country Day School were all too obvious, and not just in the wear and tear of the public school's building, or its neglected grounds. Bettina shuddered at the bars on the windows and the graffiti on a far wall.

Lily's silence spoke volumes.

The little girl's eyes stayed downcast as Susan Graham, the school's principal, came out of her office, in order to greet her newest pupil. But immediately after shaking hands and introducing herself, in a brisk, take-no-prisoners tone, Principal Graham warned, "I hope Lily is prepared to come to learn, and to be on her best behavior. Here at Lincoln, we won't tolerate even the smallest infraction. We can't afford to do so. Too much is at stake for my children."

She's like a warden who anticipates the worst from the prisoners, Bettina thought. My God, they're only children! It's not as if they're hardened criminals...are they?

Noting the concern on Bettina's face, Principal Graham added, "And by the way, our school is a drug-free zone."

"I would not have presumed otherwise," Bettina murmured.

Frightened, Lily looked up at the principal. "Does that mean I can't take my allergy pill?"

Principal Graham's incredulous look stayed on her face for quite some time before she burst out laughing. "Well, well, that certainly made my day." She held out her hand to Lily. "I'll take you to your classroom. Your teacher is Mrs. Vanderbilt. She'll encourage you to make lots of new friends."

A Vanderbilt? Well, then things can't be so bad, Bettina thought. She tapped Principal Graham on the shoulder. "I went to Wesleyan with a Vanderbilt! Her name is Bitsy— that is, Elizabeth."

Principal Graham smothered a grin. "Yes, well, Mrs. Vanderbilt's name is Liz, but I doubt she's your old school chum. Now, if you'll excuse us, I'll take Lily down the hall to her class, as I have a few more appointments waiting." She nodded toward two boys, at least eleven years old, who slumped down in their chairs.

Bettina thought, *Just like that?* I don't think so. "I'd like to walk with you, so that I might meet her teacher too."

As Bettina passed by, one of the boys nudged the other and made an obscene gesture.

She stifled the urge to box his ears.

"*BITSY?*" BETTINA'S RECOGNITION CAME OUT AS A SHOCKED gasp.

Had Principal Graham known Elizabeth Mary Vanderbilt in her heyday, she too would have mistaken her for someone else. From what Bettina could tell by Liz's cheap jeans and the resigned grimace on her now-lined face, these times were anything but easy for her old sorority sister.

In a matter of seconds, the teacher's benign stare went from curious to surprised to chagrined. Her lips followed a similar trajectory, starting with a smile that rounded out into an open mouth, before flattening into a line of disappointment. "Seriously? Bettina Connaught—*here*?"

Principal Graham patted Lily's head. "Ms. Vanderbilt, we have a new student: Lily Cross."

When Liz Vanderbilt's gaze dropped to the little girl, her lips once again raised into a smile. She proffered her hand to Lily. "Nice to meet you, Lily."

For the first time in days, Lily smiled too.

Well, this is a step in the right direction, Bettina thought.

"Let me introduce you to the rest of the class, Lily." Even as she beckoned the girl forward, over her shoulder she murmured to Bettina, "As you see, there's a lot on my plate. Unfortunately, I'll be tied up after school today and tomorrow. Why don't we catch up after school, on, say, Friday?"

Bettina, still in shock, nodded slowly, then followed Principal Graham out the door.

How the mighty have fallen, she thought to herself, as she walked out of the school.

Only when she hit Polk Street did it dawn on her that others probably thought the same about her.

Including Bitsy—make that Liz Vanderbilt.

BETTINA SPENT THE DAY AT A NEARBY COFFEE SHOP. IT WAS shabby, as were most of its other patrons. From what she could tell, a single cup of coffee allowed them to loiter all day.

I'm no better, she realized. *I've got nowhere to go either—*

No, I'm at the most important place I can be: close to my child.

She was standing at the front door when school let out for the day. Liz walked the students to the gate and watched as they made their way in various directions. Most of the children seemed to be walking home, toward the low-income housing and weekly-occupancy hotels that surrounded the school. They shuffled off either alone or in groups, but few had their parents with them.

Liz waved tentatively at Bettina, who waved back. The hesitation to do so to each other was not lost on either woman.

Lily was the last of the kindergarteners out the door. But Bettina noticed that Liz stayed at the gate even after the Connaughts walked away. When they reached the corner, Liz finally went inside. By then, the last of her charges were also out of sight.

When Bettina asked Lily how her day went, her daughter shrugged. "Most of the other kids can't read. I was bored, until Mrs. Vanderbilt let me go to the school library and check out a book." She opened her satchel and pulled out *A Bear Called Paddington*.

Bettina frowned. "But, sweetie, you already have this book at home. You read it last year."

Lily shrugged. "I know. But we also have so many of the other books in the school's library. And I had to pretend to read *something*."

My daughter is lost, Bettina thought. And so am I.

This time, when they walked by the homeless woman with the two children, Bettina slipped Lily one of the ten-dollar bills buried in her purse.

Lily handed it to the woman.

Before Bettina turned the corner, she looked back. The woman was handing off the bill to some man who seemed to morph out of the shadows of the doorway behind her.

Oh, hell, why was I so stupid? Of course, she's got a pimp! From now on, Lily needs to understand that we can't be throwing away our money anymore.

The thought of all the money she'd wasted throughout the years—including the purchase of the fourteen hundred-dollar shoes she now wore, which she never really liked anyway, made her nauseous.

She looked down at the shoes. Right then and there,

she decided they were yet another item in her wardrobe that she'd never wear again. Maybe a local consignment shop could sell them for a couple of hundred dollars. Considering how little she had in her bank account, the sooner she parted with them, the better.

She knew she should sell her handbag too. Last year, she paid an astronomical ninety-five thousand dollars for the rose-tone Hermés Scheherazade Birkin bag. It was her most expensive acquisition ever, and her proudest too, since it gave any woman who knew of its worth yet one more reason to be envious of her.

Still, she prayed it would never come to that.

If she got what she wanted out of Daniel, her prayers would be answered.

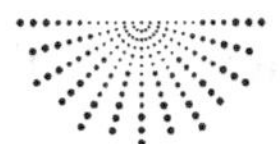

CHAPTER TEN

Friday, 7 September
9:22 a.m.

"Tell me that today isn't your birthday," Brady begged Ally.

He'd entered the kitchen with Zoe in his arms. She held chunks of his hair in her hands. At this point in her new little game, his hair was still attached to his head. He tickled her in the hope that it would stay that way, so that he could place her in her high chair.

Ally stopped mid-flip of a pancake. "Of course it isn't, silly! You already know that."

"Then why are Jillian, Lorna, and Jade standing outside, with balloons?"

Ally frowned. "I have no idea…Oh, no! Don't tell me they…"

Instead of completing the sentence, she ran to the front door, and threw it open.

In unison, her friends shouted, "Congratulations!"

She raised her head skyward and shook it. "No way! I told you I was done with the club."

"Seriously?" Lorna asked. "Do you really want Zoe to miss out on seeing which kid gets lost in the pumpkin patch this year—?"

Jade interrupted her, "And to see how long it takes for Ferguson to tear down the Fairmont's Gingerbread house—?"

"Not to mention all those academically stimulating AP classes for all of our gifted children?" Jillian teased. "I hear they've hired a Russian chess master for the Twosies. I want to see how many toddlers swallow the pawns before the instructor pulls out his hair."

"Ah, yes, good times," Ally retorted.

"And besides, now that I'm carrying twins, I'll need all the help I can get in keeping Bettina in line." Lorna patted her belly.

The others turned to her, their eyes wide with surprise. She teared up at their hugs, and congratulations.

"Ugh, guilt! You know it never works with me." Still, Ally gave Lorna a kiss on the cheek, then shrugged. "How did you pull off my reinstatement, anyway?"

Lorna laughed. "Between relaxing some of the more idiotic admission rules, going to an admissions lottery, and some sleight-of-hand on Jade's part to counter Kimberley's full-blown cheating, you got a lucky draw."

"'Lucky' isn't the word I'd use," Ally muttered. "Let me get this straight: there truly is a kinder, gentler Bettina?"

"I wouldn't go that far," Lorna admitted. "But she can only fight so many battles, and it looks like a few of her toadies are turning on her."

"To be honest, the situation is far from perfect," Jade added. "Another former member will also be making a comeback: *Kelly Overton*."

Ally whistled her surprise. "Well, I'll be darned! It'll be worth the price of admission just to see how Bettina handles that."

"You've been handed your golden ticket," Brady declared from the doorway. He was still struggling with the giggling Zoe. "So, what are you waiting for? And take your evil little spawn with you."

"Ha! You just want her out of your hair," Ally declared, as she disentangled her daughter from Brady's head. Ally patted his scalp tenderly.

He laughed. "I think you'd agree that it's something I can't afford to lose, at my age."

Seeing the other toddlers in their strollers, Zoe let loose with a gleeful squeal.

"Looks like I'm outnumbered." Ally muttered. "Okay, give me a moment to change out of my sweats, so I look worthy of the honor being bestowed upon me."

"Welcome back." Lorna hugged her tightly. "No one deserves it more."

Ally sighed. "That's what I'm afraid of."

10:05 a.m.

ONCE AGAIN, *I AM SOMEBODY*, BETTINA THOUGHT.

She saw it in the look of awe in the eyes of all the new Onesies mothers, all of whom were dressed up, as the Inaugural Play Date invitations commanded—not in so many words, but certainly implied by the event's location, the elegant James Leary Flood Mansion.

If ever Bettina needed validation of her place in San Francisco society, it was now.

Their reverence for her was mirrored in the eyes of the Twosies, Threesies, Foursies, and Fivesies replacement mothers as well—

That is, except for two Twosies moms. Kelly, the smug conniving bitch, had the audacity to grab Bettina in a death grip in front of everyone, while proclaiming, "My dearest, oldest, friend!" When her mouth was next to Bettina's ear, she murmured, "Emphasis on '*old*'."

It took all of Bettina's strength not to slap Kelly's face, right then and there. Instead, she declared in a voice loud enough for the Top Moms hovering nearby—that is, Kimberley, Mallory, and Sally—"The club hasn't been the same without you." To which she added, with a whisper: "Thank goodness. So, whatever fresh hell you plan, forget about it."

Kelly ignored her. Instead, her eyes roamed over Bettina, head to toe, but circled back to her midsection. "Ah, I see that you're pregnant again! Is it Art's?"

Bettina's smile wavered, if only for a second. Every day she checked the mirror in order to gauge the thickening of her waist, so that she might choose the right ensemble to disguise it. "Who else's could it be?" she hissed.

"You're so right. I forget that your sort of sex play—that is to say, none at all—doesn't appeal to most men."

She moved on toward the sumptuously laden refreshment table, which was being manned by Kimberley and Sally.

Kimberley looks like the cat that swallowed the canary, Bettina thought.

Kelly walked right up to Kimberley and gave her an air-kiss; it was all Bettina needed to see to realize that her accusation of Lorna regarding Kelly's lottery draw had been misplaced—this once, anyway.

At least, when Bettina's gaze met Ally Thornton's, there was no triumph there, not even the hint of barely civil coolness.

In fact, if Bettina wasn't mistaken, Ally looked downright sorry for her.

Why the nerve of her, she thought, feeling sorry for *me*.

At that moment, Bettina didn't know whom she hated more: Kelly, Lorna, or Ally.

"Ladies? Ladies, please! I must have your attention!" To make her point, Bettina tapped a fork against a crystal goblet.

All eyes went to Bettina, who graced her onlookers with a beatific smile. "I want to thank each of you for the time and effort you put toward our club, which to many of us, is as important as family." She held out her hands. "As you see, our family just got bigger, what with all the new mothers and tots added in each age group. Unlike past years, we felt it only fair that all new member applications be put into a lottery for open slots. Please, let's give a hand to all the lucky ones—our new members!"

The applause from those with a longer membership standing was tepid, as if each was thinking, *You don't know how lucky you are, not to have had to go through the same hoops as me.*

Well, too bad, Bettina thought. We must maintain the status quo. In that regard, it's see no evil, hear no evil, and above all speak no evil about PHM&T.

"Each new member will stand and introduce themselves, and their little ones, to us," Bettina continued,

"But, first things first. As in all families, there is a hierarchy. Needless to say, as the club's founder, I am at its pinnacle. At the same time, each age group has a Top Mom who helps facilitate the communication within that group. Let me introduce you to these marvelous women! Ladies, please stand as I say your name." She turned to her Top Moms. "For the Fivesies, we have Kimberley Savitch…"

Then Mallory, Sally and finally, Jade were introduced.

Afterward, Bettina beckoned the group to, "Give our Top Moms a big hand!"

The room roared its applause.

"And now, to go over some of the wonderful changes we've made to accommodate our bigger family—"

Too late, she realized she'd forgotten to mention Lorna's new leadership role, but by then she'd already launched into the process for choosing the new Onesies Top Mom, so too bad. Lorna was a big girl. She'd get over it.

LORNA STOOD BY AS BETTINA INTRODUCED THE OTHER Top Moms—

But somehow forgot to introduce her as well.

Why, she won't even look in my direction, Lorna realized. *Okay, then, two can play this game.*

"But as with any family, we must adhere to a few

rules." Seeing the worried faces on the new members, and the eye-rolls from the older ones, Bettina quickly added, "But not too, too many! In fact, this year—"

"This year, in order for the club to stay strong, it will need the tender loving care of each and every one of you," Lorna declared. She now stood side by side with Bettina.

But before Bettina could do or say anything, Lorna put her arm around Bettina's waist. "Hello, my name is Lorna Connaught, and I've had the honor of being asked by Bettina to join her as co-Chief Executive Mom of the Pacific Heights Moms & Tots Club. To that end, along with Bettina, I'd like to thank all of you for your loyalty to the club during a most difficult time."

Bettina's eyes opened wide with anger at Lorna's audacity. Her glare pierced Lorna like a laser beam.

The Top Moms turned to stare at her too. Mallory's frown reflected Bettina's, whereas Sally looked as if she'd faint from shock. From Kimberley's sly grin, it was obvious to Lorna that she enjoyed watching Bettina boil.

Jade's admiring wink gave Lorna the courage to say, "Your hard work will no longer go unrecognized, or unre-warded. To that end, the Top Moms openly invite you to review the club's rulebook, then rate each of our rules as necessary or unnecessary, with your reason for saying so. At the next meeting, one by one, we'll debate those regu-lations with an 'unnecessary' rating of fifty percent or higher, and then take a full-membership vote as to their continuation."

There was uproarious applause to Lorna's declaration.

"And now, Bettina has more good news regarding the expansion of the Top Moms Committee." She nudged her sister-in-law in the back.

Stunned, Bettina, started, "Yes…well, the expansion within our age groups gives us the opportunity to expand the Top Moms Committee as well, by three additional moms in each age group, for a total of four."

There was a smattering of claps for this as well.

"Those interested in running should put in their names, then make their case to their mommy group. Each group will take its own vote," Lorna interjected. "Now, before we move on to introductions of our new moms, are there any questions?"

One woman, way in the back, raised her hand. "I have a question for Bettina. Tell us, did you know your husband was robbing some of the club's members?"

"*What?* Did I…" Bettina's eyes opened wide. "No, of course I didn't! What do you take me for, anyway?"

Someone else yelled out, "Do you really want us to tell you?"

The remark elicited a few snickers from across the room.

Bettina shook in anger. She waited until she could hold her head high, but her eyes glistened from her tears. "If I have any fault in all this, it was in marrying a man who was able to deceive me along with so many others. I take no joy in his misdeeds. I am paying for it, dearly, both financially, with the loss of my worldly possessions; and emotionally with the loss of your respect. So, if it gives you any solace, then by all means, enjoy my comeuppance! Rejoice in my fall from grace! But do me a favor: please don't take it out on my daughter"—she patted her stomach—"or my unborn child."

A gasp went up through the room. Few had seen Bettina since news of Art's embezzlement was made public. All now duly scrutinized her still slight figure.

Lorna could only imagine how much Bettina hated being the center of attention for all the wrong reasons: Art, and a barely-there baby bump.

The silence in the room made it easy for Lorna and Jade, who was next to her, to hear Kelly lean over to Kimberley in order to murmur, "Well, what do you know! Bettina Connaught Cross gets the upper hand by playing the sympathy card."

Lorna never felt sorrier for Bettina than at that very moment. It had nothing to do with what Bettina said in her own defense, but because she might actually be defenseless against the two women who seemed united in seeing her fail.

"Did you get your kicks in blindsiding me?" Bettina snarled.

Lorna looked around. At least Bettina waited until

everyone else had cleared out of the event before confronting her.

Lorna sighed. "I wasn't the one who asked the question of your complicity in Art's crime."

"How do I know the woman who spoke up wasn't just another one of your lottery choices? Maybe putting me on the spot was her way of thanking you!"

"Snap out of it, Bettina! It was bound to happen sooner or later. And, let's face it, your woes are the elephant in every room you walk into. If the club members are ever going to trust you again, answering that question, once and for all, puts an end to it." Lorna shrugged. "And, frankly, you did so admirably. Maybe you should speak from the heart more often."

Bettina pursed her mouth into a frown. She hated to admit it, but Lorna was right. "Okay, already! I...I get it. It's just...As you can imagine, the week hasn't been an easy one, what with the raid, and Lily being kicked out of Pacific Heights Country Day School. The public school is a total disaster! And now, to boot, I have to deal with Kimberley and Kelly—"

"That's my point, exactly," Lorna retorted. "It's time you realize that I'm not the enemy. If you're in the mood to vent your wrath, I'd very much appreciate your doing so in their direction as opposed to mine."

Lorna didn't want to wait for Bettina's reply. She put Dante in his stroller and rolled him out the door.

2:33 p.m.

"Yeah, fine! Prepare to have your socks knocked off." Brady covered his iPhone with his hand when he heard the chatter of Ally, Jillian, and Jade as they walked into his house with four giggling toddlers. But then he skedaddled into his office, closing the door behind him before Oliver's shouts of "Daddy! DAD-*DEE!*" could be heard over his assurances to, "round up the ladies and come down to the Valley for a real powwow…"

He jumped off the phone quickly because Oliver was pounding on the door. He had just swooped his son up into his arms when Ally called out, "Who was that?"

"A possible investor for Life of Pie," he announced. "Owen Acworth, of Collins, Acworth and Markham. By the way, he calls you, 'the one who got away.'"

She batted her eyes at him. "Heck, had I known he was so smitten with me, I would have let him pick up Foot Fetish for the mere pittance he offered at the time."

Brady laughed. "You were smart to hold out for Bracknell Industries." He turned to Jillian. "The meeting is set for ten o'clock on Wednesday, the thirty-first. You'll need coverage for the twins."

Ally's grin faded. "Not good! Have you forgotten that PHM&T has its costume contest before the Chestnut Street Halloween Parade that afternoon? See if you can move the meeting."

He shook his head. "We can't. It almost took us an hour of flogging our calendars to come up with that date! Either Owen or Liam is out of town until then, and their partner, Teddy Collins, leaves for a two-month sabbatical the day after."

Jillian winced. "If the meeting is at ten and the parade starts at two, we may make it back from Silicon Valley in time. If Caleb can't take off from work that morning, I guess I can beg my mother." Whereas Jillian's mother was a pill, her boyfriend was truly her knight in shining armor. The tall, dark, and muscular park ranger met Jillian for the first time when he saved her daughters in their runaway stroller. Caleb also banged up her ex-husband, Scott, when he threatened to break down her front door.

Scott and Jillian were finally able to come to a truce in time for their divorce settlement. Just as importantly, Jillian and Caleb came to an understanding as to why her difficult history with Scott should never serve as a deterrent to their growing love.

"You don't have to do that! I'll be glad to take them," Jade offered. "Oliver would love it."

"That would be…super, Jade!" Jillian's telltale stutter was evident to Ally. She squeezed Jade's hand as a way of saying *thank you.*

"Ally, we'll want to go over the financial history to date one more time, just to see if they can punch holes in it." Brady paced the room excitedly, as he thought out loud. "As for the presentation, either we flip a coin as to which one of us presents financials as opposed to marketing—unless you have a preference. Seriously, it doesn't matter to me."

"Good! Then, I won't have to talk!" Relief put color back into Jillian's face.

Brady stopped in his tracks. "*Au contraire, mon amie.* You're the face of Life of Pie. You're our Colonel Sanders, our Mrs. Fields, our not-yet-famous-but-soon-to-be Amos—"

"Yeah, yeah, okay! I get it," Jillian gasped. She dropped down into a chair. "I'm…I'm just not good at public speaking."

"When I get done with you, you'll be doing TED talks, with ease," he assured her.

"I think I'm going to throw up," she muttered.

Ally slapped her hand over Brady's mouth. "We get it, Brady." She walked over to Jillian and knelt beside her. "No worries. We'll go over your presentation, line by line, so that it's second nature to you. And we'll be sure to keep it short and to the point."

"Yeah, right, gotcha." Jillian nodded her head, but the terror in her eyes was still there. "Look, I better get the girls home, so that they can take their naps." She rose to her feet, but her first step was shaky.

Jade picked up Addison for her, along with Oliver, who immediately tried to yank the little girl's hair.

Addison slapped his hand. Oliver's vexation came out in an angry howl. Immediately, Jade handed him a consolation prize: his pacifier, which he promptly stuck in his mouth.

Jillian gave Jade's cheek a peck. "Thanks for taking the girls while I'm pitching the V.C.s. You're a lifesaver."

Ally walked them to the door. "Jillian, trust me, Owen and his partners are nice people. They'll be even nicer, once they taste your pies. Literally, you'll have them eating out of your hand."

"If you say so." Jillian sighed. "I've got to go back to the shop now, to see how the baking squad is doing with the two hundred pie-lets we'll need for tomorrow's Bridal Fair."

"I'll meet you there, bright and early, with our spanking brand new Pie-Mobile, so that we can move them to our booth," Ally promised.

"Don't forget the menus, and our postcards with the contest barcode," Jillian reminded her.

Ally honored her with a thumbs-up. "Already in the van."

"What is your contest prize?" Jade asked.

"We're giving away a free pie-let carousel package to some lucky bride," Ally explained.

"Your first bridal fair!" Jade exclaimed. "How exciting!"

Jillian shrugged. "I'll take a rampaging herd of ten thousand brides over three venture capitalists with too much money and not enough knowledge of what we do any day."

"They wouldn't be taking this meeting if they didn't think we have something wonderful to show them," Ally reminded her. "See you at the shop, seven-thirty, tomorrow morning, sharp."

2:52 p.m.

As she'd done the day before, Bettina was outside Lincoln Elementary School's gate prior to the kindergarten release time. She waited ten minutes after the last of Lily's classmates sauntered out before panicking. Had they somehow missed each other? Did Lily go out another door?

Bettina hurried into the front office.

Hearing her footsteps, the school secretary looked up with a scowl. "Oh, there you are Mrs. Cross. I've been calling your cell for the past hour." She pointed to the principal's office. "Your daughter is in there."

Bettina rushed through the door. When she saw Lily's face, she gasped.

The little girl had a bruise blackening over her eye. Her mouth was puckered into a scowl, but she wasn't crying. Instead she looked down at her feet. The other two girls were around Lily's age, and were sitting in chairs against another wall. One was smaller and slighter than Lily. The other one looked twice Lily's weight.

Principal Graham stood with Liz Vanderbilt. Bettina stormed up to them. "My God, what the hell happened to my daughter?"

"As you can see, she got into a scuffle with two other students," Principal Graham began.

"A 'scuffle?'" Bettina pointed to Lily's face. "Is that what you call this? My God, if her eye has any serious damage—"

"Ms. Connaught—Bettina—Lily is fine." Liz put her hand on Bettina's arm in order to get her attention. "The school nurse has taken care of her. She'll need to ice it—"

"I presume that pronouncement is supposed to assuage my fears for her life—and any thought of a lawsuit against the school for battery and bodily harm. And what of these two little hooligans who assaulted my child? Where are their parents?"

"Kim's foster mother hasn't yet completed her shift at the diner, down the block," Liz explained. "And Sara's father will be here shortly." She pointed to the other students. "Let me point out that Lily did a little damage of her own."

Bettina had to admit she was right. One of the girls had a cut lip. The other had her hand wrapped in a bandage.

Good for Lily, Bettina thought. Still, she felt that, at this stage, she should act incensed. "I'm mortified that something like this happened. And how will you punish these future penitentiary inmates?"

"Mrs. Cross, name-calling isn't necessary—" Principal Graham admonished her.

"Maybe not, but apparently, armed guards may be in order!" Bettina held her head high. "Should I hire a few to accompany my child to school? Should I ask the mayor to call out the National Guard? You know, the governor's family and mine go back a long way—"

"Mummy," Lily tugged on her mother's skirt. "Please don't call the governor. I think I can be friends now with Li'l Kim and Sara."

It was only then that Bettina noticed that Lily was holding one of the other girls' hands.

"Oh! …Well, then…" Bewildered, Bettina realized she must at least make an attempt to be mollified. "Can the school assure me that all future disagreements will be resolved without fisticuffs?"

"What's that?" Li'l Kim asked. "Some kind of nunchucks? Tell the lady that we ain't allowed to bring weapons to school, Miss Liz!"

Liz knelt beside the girl. "She knows that, Kim. 'Fisticuffs' means fighting with your hands."

The little girl's brow wrinkled in concern. "You mean, like martial arts? Can we do karate?"

Liz sighed and shook her head. "No, honey. No sort of fighting of any kind. If you have a disagreement, you find me, and I'll straighten it out."

Bettina crossed her arms at her waist. "Why were these girls bothering my daughter, anyway?"

"Sara, why don't you answer Mrs. Connaught Cross?"

Sara slumped down even further in her seat. Finally, she shrugged. "She told us she was just as poor as us. I called her a liar, so she slapped my face." She shifted her glare to Bettina. "Like I told Miss Liz, we didn't start it, but we sure did finish it."

My daughter thinks we're as poor as these wretched souls? Oh, my God, what have I done to deserve this?

Bettina took Lily's arm and pulled her out the door. There was no way she'd let a tear fall in front of these strangers, especially not Liz Vanderbilt.

What the hell was Liz doing in some rundown public school, anyway?

As curious as Bettina was about it, she was too distraught to hang around and ask. If she can't protect my daughter, she is not someone I need to cultivate, she thought. And if it happens again, I'll make her life miserable.

"Mummy, are you mad at me?" Lily's question came out as a whisper.

They were just a few blocks from Eleanor's house. Bettina pulled over to the curb, which was fine because she wasn't ready to see her mother, whom, she knew, would want to hear about Lily's day at school.

Well, she'll certainly see the results on Lily's face, Bettina thought. Serves her right for not twisting a few of the Pacific Heights Country Day School trustees' noses out of joint, starting with that odious hag, Joanna Blunt.

Bettina took her daughter's hand. "Why would you tell those girls that you were poor?"

"Aren't we? Isn't that why we live in Grandma Connaught's basement, and all of our things are gone?"

"Not exactly…I mean, yes, we've lost a lot. But Lily, sweetie, you'll never be as poor as those children. Did you see their clothes, and their hair? One of those girls lives in a foster home—"

Lily frowned. "What's that?"

"It means she can't live with her own parents, for whatever reason."

Lily's lip trembled at the thought. "Will that ever happen to me?"

"No, of course not!" Bettina unbuckled Lily's seatbelt so that she could pull the girl onto her lap. "I'll always be here for you; I promise!"

"But Daddy promised too—and he's not!" Lily gulped down her sobs.

"Lily, he is a coward. On the other hand, we Connaughts are strong and brave. No matter what *merde* is thrown our way, we are survivors."

"Survivors." Lily nodded, savoring the word.

"No—we're more than survivors! We're *leaders*." Bettina leaned back so that Lily had to look her in the eye. "We blaze trails that others follow. They listen to us! No—no, they obey us! If not, they suffer the consequences."

"Consequences?" Lily's brow wrinkled furtively. "What sort of consequences?"

"We Connaughts set the *penalties*. We always have, and we always will." Bettina smiled grimly. She could only imagine the penalty Eleanor would lay on Pacific Heights Country Day School, in light of the injuries endured by her granddaughter.

She was happy to see that Lily was finally smiling too. Apparently, her pep talk was a big help.

Bettina started the car with a sigh. "Well, it has certainly been a *septimana horribilis!* But, all's well that ends well."

"Sep…sep…horib…a what?" Lily asked.

"That's Latin, for a 'bad week.' The first word is for week, whereas horribilis—which sounds like the word 'horrible'—describes it."

"I see," Lily murmured wanly.

Obviously, she didn't really get it. "If, for example we were having a bad year, it would be *annus horribilis*. A bad month would be *mensis horribilis*. A bad afternoon is a *meridianus*—"

"*Horribilis*, right?" Lily interjected. Her mouth twisted into a wistful pucker. "I was supposed to learn Latin at my other school," she murmured mournfully. "Will Miss Liz teach us Latin at Lincoln?"

"Doubtful," Bettina muttered. It dawned on her that perhaps Liz could be coerced to watch out for Lily, for as long as the little girl served out her time there.

As far as Bettina was concerned, it wouldn't be very long at all.

By the time she pulled Eleanor's car into the garage, she'd made up her mind that whatever Daniel Warwick wanted from her, he would get, no matter how degrading it might be for her.

It was her hope that she'd enjoy it, but after her *meridianus horribilis* playing bottom to Andy Hepburn, she doubted it.

10:53 p.m.

"ONE HUNDRED AND NINETY-SEVEN, ONE HUNDRED AND ninety-eight, one hundred and ninety-nine…TWO HUNDRED!" Jillian slid the last of the mini-pies into the portable catering rack. Bright and early tomorrow, she and Ally would load it onto the Life of Pie van for tomorrow's bridal fair, along with twenty carousel stands.

It had been a long day. She was bone-tired and ready to go home.

To her babies.

To her man.

The last time she'd seen him was as she was running out the door after putting the twins down for their nap.

Usually, her day started at five in the morning. While Caleb and the twins slept, she'd shower quickly, then hop into a T-shirt, yoga pants, and zip-up sweater before going out the door. She'd jog the least steep route from her home, on Pacific near the Presidio, to the pie shop, on Union Street. There, with her two sleepy-eyed baking assistants, she'd knead dough, chop fruit, and blend her custom fillings with the variety of spices that went into the mouthwatering pies that had her rabid patrons lining up outside the shop door as early as seven in the morning.

Caleb's shift as a park ranger began at eleven in the morning, and he was home by seven o'clock. By then, the girls were fed, bathed, and put to bed, leaving Jillian and Caleb with a little adult time.

It was the best part of her day.

They spent it making love. Sometimes, they took their time, exploring the parts of each other's bodies that, with encouraging fingers and tongue, were apt to elicit tingles, shivers, sighs, moans, and best of all deep, satisfying orgasms. At other times, their loving-making was frenzied, as if their lust could only be quelled by the quick and dirty give and take that can only be offered up in complete abandonment of time and place.

Usually by nine-thirty, they were asleep in each other's arms.

That routine was not the case tonight, however. The bridal fair meant double duty.

Still, if tomorrow went well, they'd sell lots of pies for lots of weddings.

The harsh screech of the buzzer alerted her that someone was standing outside of Life of Pie's front door.

She sighed. She was there alone, and had been so since her sales clerks closed up shop at seven. She looked out the see-through mirrored window.

It was Caleb. He had a concerned look on his face.

Oh no. What's wrong?

Jillian ran to the front door, fumbling with the locks until they opened. "The twins! Is something wrong? Oh, my God—"

"No, honey! Calm down. They're sound asleep, and Ally is up at the house, babysitting." He stroked her face. "I'm sorry. I didn't mean to scare you. But…well, I have something to show you."

"Now? But it's almost midnight—"

He put a finger to her lips in order to hush her. "Trust me on this, Jill."

She could tell by his voice that he wasn't going to take no for an answer.

She lived to say yes to him, always.

She nodded and went to the back to grab her keys. As she locked the front door, she warned him, "This better be worth my missing out on an extra hour of sleep."

He smiled without saying a word. But he took her hand in his, as if he never wanted to let her go.

That was fine by her.

CALEB DROVE THROUGH THE PRESIDIO TO THE OLD OFFICER'S Club, which backed up into the wooded hills that climbed up into the stately neighborhood of Presidio Heights.

Although the building was locked up, someone was out front.

Caleb patted Jillian's hand. "Follow me."

He waved at the man, who then hopped out of the truck cab. She had no choice but to do the same.

The man threw something at Caleb: apparently, a small ring of keys.

Caleb caught it with one hand. "Thanks Jeff. Hey, come over and meet my girlfriend, Jillian." Caleb nudged Jillian forward. "Jillian, this is my boss and the Presidio's head ranger, Jeff Prescott."

Jeff shuffled over. "Pleased to meet you, Jillian." His head to toe scan ended in a knowing grin.

"You too," she said, blushing. "I hope we aren't intruding."

"Not at all."

Caleb winked at Jeff. "Thanks, guy, for doing me this little favor."

Jeff nodded. "Any time."

Caleb waited until Jeff strolled down the hill before unlocking the front door.

The only light emanating from inside came from a staircase all the way in the back of the building, beyond the cavernous reception area.

By now, Jillian was totally stymied. "Caleb, what's this all about?"

It was too dark to see his face. But, whatever doubts she had dissolved in the depth of his kiss.

His large hand took hers, and led her inside.

With him at my side, I'll never be scared, ever again, she thought.

THE DOOR AT THE VERY TOP OF THE STAIRCASE LED OUT ONTO the building's rooftop. All of San Francisco Bay—Angel Island, the Golden Gate Bridge, and the Marin Headlands beyond—could be viewed under an indigo sky puckered with glittering stars.

Laid out on a plaid picnic blanket was a veritable feast, lit by a Coleman lantern: blackened salmon sandwiches, tiny roasted red potatoes, and a green salad. A bottle of champagne sat in an ice bucket, although considering the brisk night air, it would have easily stayed chilled without the ice.

Caleb knelt on the blanket, pulling Jillian down with him. He took the bottle in his hand. When he popped the cork, the champagne's spray caused Jillian to duck. Her laughter echoed into the night, causing a few of Telegraph Hill's celebrated parrots to squawk as they flew out of the neighboring Eucalyptus trees.

Beside the ice bucket were two champagne flutes. Quickly, Caleb poured the frothy liquid into one, and handed it to her. She waited as he poured a glass for himself, staring at the shimmering gold liquid in her flute. Suddenly, she noticed that something was swirling around in it. As it separated from the bubbles, it floated to the bottom of the glass—

A diamond ring.

She cried so hard that her tears plopped into her glass, making the bubbles float even more furiously.

He put down the bottle so that he might brush away the dampness on her cheek. "I hope those are happy tears." His voice cracked with emotion. "It was my great-grandmother's wedding ring. It was supposed to have arrived three days ago, but it somehow got lost in the mail."

So, that's why he's been so upset, Jillian realized.

He sifted the bubbly carefully through his fingers, until the ring fell out of the glass. "Jillian Frederick, I hope you'll consent to marry me. If not, I may jump off this roof."

She was gasping so hard that she couldn't answer. Instead, she clutched him harder with her free hand.

She pulled him toward her in order to kiss him.

When their lips parted, she whispered, "Nothing could make me happier than to be your wife. I'm home as long as you are there."

"And you are my family," he vowed solemnly.

By the time they were ready to eat their food, it was cold.

It didn't matter. They were already sated.

CHAPTER ELEVEN

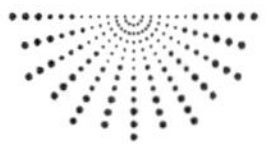

Saturday, 8 September
11:23 a.m.

"Too frothy…too frilly…too 'Lady Di,'…that one is a maybe…too old fashioned…" Jillian paused, then gasped. "Ooh! I *love* that one! Talk about giving the bride a Pippa bum! Better me than my bridesmaids, right?"

Enviously, Jillian pointed to the model who was hitting the San Francisco Bridal Fair's elevated fashion runway in a backless floor-length long-sleeved silk sheath wedding dress. With each stride, the gown's back slit emphasized the model's toned derriere.

"Hey, watch it! As one of your future bridesmaids, I shouldn't be denied the chance to look sexy too!" Pointedly, Ally's gaze went to Jillian's backside. "If it's the bridal gown you choose, you'll certainly have no problem carrying it off. Caleb won't be able to keep his eyes off of you."

Jillian blushed, even as she offered yet another bride-to-be a fork, along with one of the two hundred scrumptious pie-lets from the dessert carousels.

Considering the popularity of their booth, Ally's prediction that they'd be out of pie even before lunchtime, seemed to be on target. All morning long, waves of women—most of them there with their mothers or girlfriends, but some with chagrined fiancés—flowed through the Fort Mason Pavilion, seeking the perfect gown, the perfect ring, and the perfect food for their pending nuptials.

As far as Jillian was concerned, life was perfect as is. Or, as she blissfully recalled, "For the past month, I thought his nervousness meant he was falling out of love with me, only to discover he was worried the engagement ring he had for me was going to be too tight, because it was his great-grandmother's." She held it up so that Ally could admire it. "As it turns out, it's a perfect fit!"

Ally held her hand closer in order to get a good look. "It's a beautiful setting—so intricate!"

Jillian nodded happily. "His great-grandparents bought it before the Great Depression…" Her voice trailed off.

Ally looked up. Noting Jillian was almost pop-eyed, she followed her friend's gaze—

Directly into the eyes of Jillian's ex-husband, Scott Frederick.

He was with Victoria and their infant son, who they called Scott Victor—Scott Jr. for short.

At the exact same time, Scott did a double-take at seeing Jillian. He nudged Victoria, who was cooing to Scotty.

Victoria leaned in to hear what he had to say. A second later, she was staring straight at Jillian and Ally. Tentatively, she waved at the woman whose husband she stole.

Jillian took a deep breath, then waved back.

"That's mighty big of you," Ally murmured.

"Hell yeah, it is. And so is the ring on my finger—which, by the way, is twice the size of the ring Scott found in some Cracker Jack box."

Ally laughed hard enough to double over. Finally, she gasped. "Did you think you'd see them here?"

"I haven't even had time to think of my own wedding." Jillian shrugged. "Besides, our divorce won't be final until early November. Hey, more power to them." Suddenly, Jillian's eyes widened. "Oh, my God! I hope Victoria and I don't choose the same gown to wear down the aisle—or the same wedding date!"

By the time Scott and Victoria made their way over to the booth, Ally was sufficiently recovered from her giggle fit in order to put on a serious face for the future brides who had questions about the cost of the carousels, and available flavors.

She would have much preferred to listen in on Jillian and her ex, but the way Ally figured it, Jillian would tell her everything anyway, the moment they were out of earshot, so it was a win-win all the way around.

"THIS ONE IS PRETTY GOOD!" VICTORIA TOOK A FORKFUL OF Jillian's newest pie—lemon-lime mango—and fed it to Scott.

Jillian kept the smile on her face, but she'd be damned if she'd let them walk away before signing up for a carousel of the pies for, as Scott put it as he rolled his eyes, "the wedding of the century. Two hundred guests, at least. We're taking over the St. Francis Yacht Club. Victoria's father is a member."

Victoria smiled and shrugged. "The view is to die for. It's been a dream of mine since I was a child."

"When is the big event?" Ally asked innocently, but in truth, her question was anything but.

"Thanksgiving weekend. It's the only time we can gather both families, what with Victoria's parents coming in from Vermont on the Sunday prior." Scott glanced sideways at Jillian when he said this, just in time to see her wince. "Ha! Sorry, Jilly. Forgot that you didn't exactly get along with my mother. But, in this case, it should be fun, since Mom and Victoria actually like each other."

"No need to apologize." Jillian winked at Victoria. "She's no longer my problem."

"Good to hear," Victoria assured her with a laugh, and her signature on a Life of Pie event contract, "since we'll need twenty carousels for the wedding, and we want to make sure none are poisoned."

"But of course, they'll be fine," Ally bristled.

On the other hand, Jillian practically turned white.

Back in the spring, when she and Scott were still at odds over their divorce, Victoria purchased a chocolate cherry apricot pie for his birthday. Jillian was angry enough to crush Pedia-Lax into the filling.

Victoria ended up eating most of the pie—and immediately went into labor. Scotty's delivery was premature—but not because of the laxative. As it turned out, the laxative actually saved both their lives.

Neither Scott nor Victoria found out about Jillian's connivance. Still, Jillian was haunted by it, and vowed to resolve her issues with her ex.

Her way of making it up to him was to give in to his plea that she give him a copy of a digital file that would clear Victoria of the crime of making an illegal mutual fund purchase for one of Scott's clients—in fact, Brady Pierce—in Scott's name.

Jillian, Scott, and Victoria weren't exactly friends, but for the sake of Amelia, Addison, and Scotty, all three adults now did their best to get along.

"We'll do everything we can to make your dessert a

big hit." Jillian's sincerity brought a genuine smile to Victoria's lips.

"Thank you, Jillian." Victoria's smile was sincere. "Only one request: no chocolate cherry apricot! It may be Scott's favorite, but I've lost my taste for that particular flavor."

Ally buried her smile behind an open menu rather than laugh out loud at Jillian's bright red blush.

The applause from the runway garnered Scotty's attention, as well as his mother's. As Victoria watched the runway show, Scott leaned in over the counter. "Hey, Jillian, Victoria has her heart set on joining your moms-and-tots club. Think you can put in a good word for her and Scotty?"

"Hmmm…well, sure, I'll do my best. But I don't know if my word will carry much weight, since the club's admission selection just went to a lottery system for all new applicants."

"What a shame. For some reason, I thought it had to do with who you knew." He shrugged. "Come on, Jilly, be honest: you'd give her a leg up if you could, right?"

"I have no reason to lie to you," Jillian declared. "Or, for that matter, to hurt the chances for the twins' half-brother."

"Okay, duly noted—*I get the point*! I didn't mean to ruffle your feathers—" Suddenly, Scott paused.

Jillian realized why: he'd noticed the ring on her finger.

Scott stared at it, mesmerized. Finally, he said, "Congratulations. Have you set the date?"

She shrugged. "In the spring, maybe the summer."

"He's a very lucky man." Scott hesitated, then held out his hand. "I may not have shown it at the time, but I want you to know that I'll always cherish our years together, Jillian. I wish you my best."

"Thank you, Scott." She squeezed his hand. "That means a lot to me."

Still, Scott's grimace reflected his uneasiness at the notion of her happily ever after—

No, something else: remorse, perhaps. Or maybe regret for what could have been?

I'm imagining it, Jillian reminded herself. What is done is done.

At that moment, the booth was inundated by a group of brides, all wanting to sample the pies. By the time Jillian looked up again, Scott and Victoria were gone.

1:21 p.m.

Bettina purposely timed her arrival so that she was twenty minutes late to Daniel's hotel suite in the Fairmont. In dom/sub foreplay, a dom's late arrival would have her anxious sub wetting his black latex bondage chaps, whereas a sub who dared to do so could expect the whip applied with a heavy hand.

Considering she still hadn't figured out who was to be the dom and the sub in this relationship, Bettina was taking an awful chance.

In any event, she'd come prepared for either role. Her breasts, fuller because of her pregnancy, were barely contained in the lacy pink push-up bra she wore under her low-cut candy-apple red leather jacket. Beneath the tight matching pants was a pink lace thong. Four-inch red stilettos completed her ensemble.

Just in case it was needed, albeit she doubted so, Bettina carried a red leather flogger in her valise.

Before entering, she texted Daniel: *I'm here.*

His response was, simply: *Room 410*

She sauntered to the elevator as if she had all the time in the world, all the while praying that this would be over quickly.

THE DOOR WAS OPEN A CRACK.

Hmm, quite a quandary. A dom would enter, walk up to the sub, and crack him across the face for not being there to greet her on hands and knees. However, were she playing the sub, she would knock tentatively, then wait for his command as to how she should enter (more than likely, crawling on hands and knees).

She took the safe route: she knocked.

"Come on in," Daniel replied, somewhere deep within the lush recesses of the hotel suite.

Bettina took a deep breath, then pushed through the door.

Daniel sat in the suite's dining room. He was reading one of the many files stacked on the table. He wore jeans, with a crewneck sweater over a button-down shirt. His long legs were stretched out. She noticed that he wore loafers, but no socks.

A plate of uneaten sandwiches was on the sideboard, along with a full coffee service.

Bettina frowned, confused. *What the hell is this, anyway, tea and crumpets?*

Noting the shock on her face, he murmured, "Bettina, are you ready to begin?"

Slowly, Bettina nodded. "Yes…No! I mean…um…Why exactly am I here again?"

"To go over my case files on Art. Why?" His eyes swept over her—

Then, quickly, he looked away.

Suddenly she felt a draft at her chest. She looked down as well to see that the top buttonhole of her jacket had popped open, exposing even more of her breasts, along with her bra.

Daniel's eyes stayed on his file, but he couldn't hide his grin.

Bettina turned so that he couldn't see that her face was

as red as her suit. Grasping the button, she fumbled to stuff it back through the buttonhole—

But instead, it popped off, dropping onto the thick antique carpet.

She looked down at it, as if mesmerized.

She felt a tap on her shoulder. She didn't turn back around. Instead, meekly, she said, "Yes?"

Daniel had taken off his sweater, and was handing it to her. "If you take off the jacket and slide into this, I can sew that button back on for you."

"You…know how to do it?"

He chuckled. "Learned it from my mother. She said, 'I don't care if you are a boy. If you want nice things, you need to know how to take care of them.' The hotel put a travel sewing kit in the sideboard. It should only take a minute. I figure if you can keep from any heavy breathing during our meeting, you'll make it home intact."

"Our…meeting?" She didn't face him, so he couldn't see the relief in her face. Apparently, though, he heard it in her voice, because he replied. "Ms. Connaught Cross… I'm sorry, exactly what did you think was to take place here?"

Bettina turned around before swapping out his sweater for her jacket. When she faced him again, she wasn't smiling. "To be honest with you, Mr. Warwick, when you use terms like, 'play ball' and 'cozy up to me' and 'deliver the goods"…well, you can just imagine what I thought."

His brow furrowed for a moment. But, then, the light bulb went on.

"Oh, I see! You presumed that, having seen Art's 'closet of pain' as it were, I'd have questioned your virtue, found it lacking, and sexually exploit you. Am I right?"

She shrugged. "Something along those lines, yes."

"Mrs. Connaught Cross…Bettina, I'm sorry about that! Truly, I am." He patted her arm gently. "Of course, being married for eight years to that son of a bitch, Art, it's easy to imagine how you might have gotten the impression that all men are sadistic abusers. But let me state, here and now, for the record: I will never take advantage of you—"

She was touched. At the same time, she was somewhat disappointed.

"—because it would only damage the investigation." He held the button up to the light in order to examine it.

"You're only concerned about *the investigation*?"

"As I just explained, I care enough about you to want to put him behind bars. Not just to retrieve the money he stole, but so that he'll never hurt you again. I can't even imagine the number of bruises, emotional and otherwise, he gave you over the years. In any event, I feel your pain —metaphorically speaking, of course."

Oh…shit. He thinks Art was the dom.

Bettina blushed. "The S and M stuff—look, seriously, that just started this year! *I swear*."

Daniel put a finger on her lips to hush her up. "You

don't have to make excuses for him. Bettina, there is no way I'll ever let him hurt you, ever again. *I mean that.*"

"You…won't?" Her question came out in a squeak.

"Of course not!" He took both her hands in order to settle her gently on the couch beside him. "I just don't get it. Why would a man abuse someone as sweet and as accomplished as you, especially the mother of his child?"

"Art *is* an asshole…I mean, in so many other ways—"

"I'm glad to hear you say so."

"You are?" she asked warily.

"Yes, because it's the first step to your recovery as an abused wife."

"But, I'm not…" Bettina's mouth snapped shut. If allowing him to think that Art beat her black and blue got her what she wanted most—the life she'd once had—then by all means, she could play the victim.

My God, he's right! I *am* the victim, she told herself. Art is off sunning himself on some island while I'm fending off derelicts on my way to dropping off our little girl at a ghetto school.

Prison would do him good, she decided—and the sooner, the better. She stood up, lifting him off the couch with her. "What do we need to do to bring Art to justice?"

He smiled. "I need you to answer my questions as honestly as you can about everything you know about him. For example, his work colleagues, old acquaintances, even any old high school buddies you can think of. I want you to remember if he mentioned a place where he wanted to retire, or his most memorable vacation spots. Does he speak any other languages? Does he prefer hot weather to cold? And…well…" Daniel grimaced, then added, "Look, Bettina—I hate to bring up bad memories, but if he has sexual peccadillos worth noting—"

Talk about opening a can of worms.

She choked so hard with laughter that she shed tears.

He was so taken aback that, instinctively, he took her in his arms.

As she melted into them, the thought came to her:

If I play this right, I'll get back my things.

Wiping away her tears, she murmured, "Let's get started."

Daniel probed and prodded her—metaphorically speaking.

And Bettina loved every minute of it:

Playing the innocent, that is.

Frankly, pulling up every memory she had of Art was cathartic, if only to remind her how truly despicable he was.

She divulged every client he'd ever called "pig," or "asshole" or "whore." She brought up the assistants he labeled "dumb broads," and the ones he muttered were, "sweet pieces of ass."

"So, what you're saying is that he might have had sex with the latter?" Daniel asked.

Bettina sighed laconically. "I wouldn't doubt it in the least."

He nodded as he jotted down their names.

She assured him that Art was ignorant about languages. "In fact, he made our Guatemalan maid's life miserable by screaming at her whenever he saw even the faintest shadow of a sweat stain on his dress shirts," she pointed out. "He was a terror to the doorman too, so I wouldn't waste time looking for him anywhere south of the border. Perhaps Canada?"

Daniel scribbled a note. "His lineage…Welsh descent?"

Bettina nodded. "So he claimed. But I know for a fact that he had a couple of German cousins."

Again, Daniel took pen to pad. "Do you remember what city in Germany?"

"Where is the headquarters for Mercedes-Benz?" she mused. "I presume it's the same place, since one of them worked there. He was always begging the poor guy to buy a Maybach for him, and ship it over here—claiming he'd pay him back. The man was too smart to trust him."

"If only the rest of his victims had those instincts." Daniel handed her a file. "Art left these selfie photos on an old laptop in the bottom of his bedroom closet. Do you recognize any of these women?"

With trembling hands, Bettina opened the file.

Whores, all of them.

In some of the photos, they clung seductively to stripper poles, somewhere deep in the recesses of red-hued rooms, where the strobe lights cast long shadows on men who, with eyes upturned, drooled into their rocks glasses.

Then there were the selfies he'd taken with women who were sprawled across the tufted back seats of stretch limousines. In most cases, the tarts were dressed to the nines, their eyes glazed over from whatever drink was sloshing out of the martini glasses they held in one hand, even as they played with Little Art with the other.

Still, even the naked ones were at least wearing Louboutin heels and Tiffany necklaces.

One of the naked ones—porcelain-skinned, big-breasted, and platinum-haired—was wearing something other than heels: a pair of earrings that looked all too familiar to Bettina.

"Why, that son of a bitch gave her my earrings!" Bettina gasped. "And all this time, he let me believe I'd lost those somehow!"

Daniel stared down at the woman in the picture. Something about her made him lean in for a closer look. "Ha! Well, what do you know."

Bettina looked up sharply. "You recognize her?"

"Unfortunately, yes. It's Liesel Wenstrom. She's a Swedish film star. Her husband is a Russian mobster who launders his money here in the United States."

"I don't get it! Why would a mobster's moll be in the back of a limo with my whore-mongering husband?" Bettina held the photo closer for a better look before tossing it on the floor. "Don't answer that! In fact, you have my permission to post it on the Internet. Maybe her hubby will see it and rub them both out. It should save the American taxpayers a pretty penny, keeping him out of some Club Fed."

"Quite frankly, we'd prefer him in lock-up if it leads to the reparation of the funds he stole from his unsuspecting clients," Daniel pointed out.

"Duly noted. I'll try not to throttle him if he shows up some day—which I doubt, considering the many whores his ill-gotten billions can obviously buy him." Bettina shrugged. "I wish I could help you further, Daniel, but let's face it, his kind of trash isn't invited to sit on the trustee boards of the opera and…"

And then she saw her:

Kelly.

The picture was taken on a playground—Lafayette Park, from the look of it. From what Bettina could see, in the foreground, Kelly, dressed primly in sleek slacks and a pea coat, made fish lips at the camera, as if she didn't have a care in the world. In the background, Kelly's toddler son, Wills, was in an infant swing, pushed by Lily.

The photo must have been taken last fall because Lily wore a coat that was much too tight for her now.

Bettina knew Art once had an affair with Kelly. Unbeknownst to the other Top Moms, it was the reason Bettina had her kicked out of the club in the first place.

It was also the reason for her physically abusive sex life with Art. He had enjoyed getting walloped by Kelly.

When confronted by Bettina, Kelly turned over the paddle to her, literally.

At first, it was satisfying to counter her emotional hurt with his physical pain. But if she were to be honest with herself, it had never made up for his infidelity.

Ironically, their kinky sex play left her feeling emptier than before.

He deserted me long before he walked out the door and went into hiding, she realized.

"Are you okay?" Daniel asked gently. "Do you know this woman?"

"Yes…but she's not important."

Just saying it out loud put so much into perspective, including the need to move on with her life.

The first step of that journey began with putting Art behind bars.

Suddenly, she sat up straight. "Switzerland," she proclaimed.

Daniel looked up from Kelly's photo. "I beg your pardon?"

"Art loves to ski. And, enough people there speak English that he doesn't have to learn their language. More to the point, he'd insist on being close to his money, which means all of the tropical offshore banking capitals are out, since he sunburns too easily."

"Would he consider plastic surgery?" Daniel asked.

She snorted. "In a minute! Especially if, by some miracle, it made him look like George Clooney."

Now, Daniel was laughing too.

He patted her hand.

She leaned in and kissed him.

He didn't pull away. In fact, he moved in closer.

The kiss lasted longer than it should. Still, it was not long enough for Bettina.

He sighed as he leaned away from her.

"You don't want me to jeopardize this case," he warned her.

"You're right. I don't." She stood up and reached for her valise, then realized that she was still in his sweater. "Um…Daniel, can you turn around? I need to change into my jacket."

He did as he was told, facing the window instead.

Bettina pulled off the sweater and put on her jacket with its button, now tightly secured. Since his back was turned, she took a moment to look at him unobserved. She loved his height, and the broadness of his shoulders, and the thickness of his neck. Without his sweater, she noticed the gun holster in the small of his back.

Sadly, it dawned on her: *If need be, he'll shoot Art.*

She nudged him with the sweater. "Feel free to call me

if you need anything else," she said, as a way of saying goodbye.

"Bettina, listen…" He struggled to find the right words. Finally, he sighed. "You'll want to take this with you."

He walked to the hotel desk and picked up something—

Brochures of some sort. He wasn't smiling when he handed a couple of them to her.

They announced an auction.

As she rifled through one, she saw that many of her possessions were showcased. The brochure also included photos of her now-empty penthouse condo. Its listing price was a steal for the sky-high San Francisco realty market. The date of the auction was sometime in March.

Oh, my God, she thought. The horse sculpture! If anyone else should get ahold of it and figure out the release on it, I'll have no leverage at all with the other Top Moms. "Please, Daniel, at least give me Lily's horse sculpture! She made it, so of course it had nothing to do with Art! And besides, I promised her—"

His face hardened into a scowl. "It's on page forty-five."

She tore at the pages until she found it—

Yes, there it was.

And, apparently, it had been appraised, because it was attributed to its real artist, Jeff Koons.

Bettina's eyes shifted from the page to Daniel's face.

His stony glare made her wince.

He crossed his arms at his chest. "No more lies, Bettina. Tell me the real reason you want it so badly."

"I...I bought it for Lily. With funds from my trust, so Art has nothing to do with it."

He leaned in, so that they were eye to eye. "Is that all?"

She hesitated.

In that second, she almost convinced herself that she could trust him about the files buried in the base of the figurine. But then she realized he'd have to read them in order to verify that she was telling the truth: that they had nothing to do with Art.

If he read them, he'd realize how far she'd go to retain her rock-solid hold on the women who despised her most.

He'd realize what a bitch she really was.

So instead, she nodded.

He shrugged. "It's a very valuable piece of art. Its sale will go a long way toward making restitution to your husband's victims."

She frowned. "But—but you said if I helped you, I'd get my things!"

"You are helping, believe me. And if we catch him between now and then—"

"But what if you don't? It's not my fault if he turns out to be smarter than everyone who is trying to catch him—including you!"

"Bettina, listen to me. If we locate him based on any

information you've given me, I can release your possessions to you. In fact, you'll be eligible for a reward. But I can't guarantee any of it will happen prior to the auction. I'm sorry. That's just the way it is."

She wanted to smack him silly with the brochures, for getting her hopes up about everything, but then she remembered that she was no longer a sadist.

Instead, she stuffed the brochures into her valise.

Old habits die hard, she thought, as she stormed out the door. Here's hoping old husbands do too.

CHAPTER TWELVE

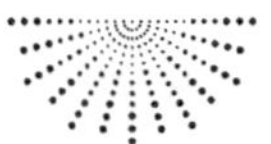

Friday, 14 September
1:22 p.m.

"—A BIG ROUND OF APPLAUSE FOR ALL FOUR OF THE NEW Onesies Top Moms! I'm sure they'll make wonderful additions to the club's steering committee," Lorna proclaimed to the PHM&T member body. "This past week of campaigning really paid off, ladies! Well done!"

The accommodating shouts of cheers echoed through the Moscone Recreation Center's auditorium. The women in question blushed at the shouts cheering them on. However, when one of them—Shoshanna Murdock— waved back, Bettina's attempt to pin an apricot-hued rosebud corsage on Shoshanna's chest resulted in a pained yelp.

Bettina's sigh may have been loud, but it was also all

too obviously insincere. "Oopsy, my bad! But seriously, Shoshanna, you've got no one to blame but yourself. Goodness, is that a tear? Of joy, I hope, for the honor of joining the committee. Now, sidle over, why don't you, so that we can move on to the next winners."

She turned to Lorna and rolled her eyes to indicate *all's well that ends well, let's get this show on the road.*

Lorna's resignation was a shake of her head. Still, she rallied on. "And, now it's time to announce the three mothers with the most votes in the Twosie group! Ladies, as Bettina calls your name, please take your position with Twosie Top Mom Jade Pierce!"

She threw out her left arm in order to acknowledge the current committee members: Jade, Sally, Kimberley, and Mallory.

As the three women grinned and nodded to the crowd, Mallory muttered to Kimberley, "Savor these last few seconds of being leaders of the pack. Thanks to our fearless co-leaders, your power is about to be cut to a quarter of what it used to be."

Kimberley shrugged. She had an ace up her sleeve, and it was about to be played.

Bettina swapped Lorna's microphone and the winners' list for the corsage basket. No doubt, the relieved sighs heard throughout the crowd were in response to Shoshanna's whimpering.

"Will the following people please join us on the stage," Bettina muttered unenthusiastically. "Jillian Frederick,

Ally Thornton, and…Kelly Bryant Overton." She didn't wait for the applause to die down between the names. Perhaps that was a good thing, considering the guttural growl in which she spat out Ally's name. Worse yet, she gagged on her shout-out to Kelly.

Lorna was much gentler with the corsages. In fact, she hugged Jillian and Ally after pinning them.

Bettina did notice that Lorna lost her smile when she reached Kelly, and after pinning her corsage, Lorna neglected to hug her.

Instead, Lorna walked over to Bettina, put her arm around her, and declared gaily, "Now, onto the winners who will join Mallory as the other Threesies Top Moms…"

For the first time since Lorna had entered the Connaughts' rarified universe, Bettina was grateful to have her sister-in-law at her side.

"WHAT SAY WE LET BYGONES BE BYGONES?" KELLY suggested innocently to Bettina. "You know, bury the hatchet." Her voice was low enough that the other Top Moms couldn't overhear her.

Bury the hatchet? Don't tempt me, Bettina thought. Otherwise you'll find it in the center of your back.

Until that very moment, the first full meeting of the new year's PHM&T Top Moms committee had been a success—which, to Bettina's way of thinking, meant that Ally Thornton's questions to her were polite and deferential, and that Kelly had sat meekly, with her mouth shut.

She waited until the few women left in the auditorium —Lorna, along with Jade and Kimberley, who she'd corralled to help her fold and stack the chairs—were out of earshot before finally retorting, "If I were holding a grudge, you'd never have been invited back into the club."

"Good to hear," Kelly purred. "You know, Bettina, I don't hold any grudges against you, either. Frankly, I feel sorry for you. Art left you in quite a little pickle, no pun intended." She looked down at Bettina's barely-there baby bump.

"I don't need your pity," Bettina bristled. "And I certainly don't need your condescension…" It perturbed her to no end that, all of a sudden, Kelly seemed preoccupied. Why was she staring off into space?

Bettina snapped her fingers in front of Kelly's nose. "Hello, Kelly? Are you listening? My God, woman, you started this conversa—" Instinctively, Bettina turned to see what had caught the other woman's attention.

It was the man at the door: Andy Hepburn.

He scanned the room, as if looking for someone.

The Twosies' soccer session had ended over an hour ago, Bettina thought. What is he still doing here?

When his eyes fell on her, she blushed. Her hand

patted her stomach at the thought that her child might indeed be his—

But no, it wasn't Bettina who had his eye. Kelly's sly smile and slight nod was proof of that.

Now he belongs to Kelly? Bettina's stomach lurched at the thought of the two of them together.

Suddenly, the thought hit her: Has he told her about me?

Still, she held it together while Kelly blathered out some excuse to get away—something about getting little Wills home for a bath and a nap.

Then she bundled the crawling little boy in her arms, and strolled out the door.

Bettina walked toward the window. She watched until they came into view. As she presumed, Andy walked Kelly to her car. As she strapped her son into his car seat, Andy had the audacity to cup her bum.

After closing the passenger door, Kelly slammed him up against the car, and put her hand between his legs.

The pain caused him to flinch.

And yet, the smile stayed on his face—

Even as they kissed.

Bettina was just as confused as she was angry. *Who the hell is the dom in that relationship, anyway?*

Oh, what do I care, she thought miserably. Those two pervs deserve each other!

She headed for the door, all the while digging in her Hermés handbag for her keys. She sighed as she heaved the handbag onto a table, and turned it upside down. Along with the keys and her makeup, the two U.S. Marshal auction brochures tumbled out.

Bettina stared at them. Then, angrily, she tossed them into the trash bin by the door.

For once, she hoped it was Art's child she carried in her womb.

AH, SO NOW SHE KNOWS.

The look of shock and anger on Bettina's face was enough to make Kimberley giggle out loud.

Lorna turned and frowned. "What's so funny?"

"Oh…nothing," Kimberley assured her. With as much innocence as she could muster, she scanned the room. "I think that takes care of things, don't you?"

Lorna looked around. All the chairs were folded, and all the tables were against the wall. Jade and Jillian were on the floor with Dante, Oliver, Zoe, Addison and Amelia. "Thanks for your help." She waved goodbye to Kimberley, and then walked toward Jillian and Jade, to grab Dante and say goodbye.

The moment Lorna's back was turned, Kimberley stuck her hand in the trash can. It was worth reaching beneath a few dirty disposable diapers deposited during the day's proceedings to see what Bettina had tossed away:

A couple of the U.S. Marshal's auction brochures for Bettina's possessions!

She picked one up, flipped through it—

And did a double-take: *Bettina's horse statue stared her in the face.*

When she saw the opening bid, she blanched: twelve thousand dollars.

If I could raise that, it would put that bitch in her place, once and for all. Kimberley's heart pounded so hard in her chest that she almost fainted.

Suddenly, she felt someone watching her: Lorna.

She was too excited to attempt nonchalance. Instead, she hurried out the door.

AFTER WAVING GOODBYE TO KIMBERLEY, LORNA PICKED UP Dante and her purse, and said goodbye to Ally, Jillian, and Jade.

Whereas Zoe, the twins, and Ollie seemed energized after their soccer workout, Dante's yoga class had worn him out.

I wish he'd been able to play with the others, she thought. But no—only baby steps for my little man.

She turned around in time to see Kimberley pick something out of the trash can by the door.

A couple of things, actually—brochures of some sort.

One was smudged badly. Kimberley tossed it back, but kept the other. She flipped through it—

Until something stopped her cold. Whatever she read made her smile jubilantly.

But, when she looked up and saw Lorna staring at her, she scurried out the door.

Lorna walked to the trash can. Careful to avoid the messy diapers and other refuse, she picked up the one remaining catalog.

As she turned its pages, she realized why Kimberley was so gleeful: it was filled with Bettina's antiques, collectables, and other personal items.

Poor Bettina, Lorna thought. A pregnancy was hard enough. The last thing she needed was to have Kimberley gunning for her too.

CHAPTER THIRTEEN

Monday, 13 October

11: 23 a.m.

"Bettina, I insist that you quit moping around the house."

Eleanor's command came with a prod that roused Bettina from the chaise lounge beside her mother's pool. She had been daydreaming that she and Lily were living on some tropical island resort—her favorite, the Rosewood Little Dix Bay, the British Virgin Islands. There, no one knew them. Best of all, no one bothered them. Certainly not Lorna, who would welcome her departure.

And certainly not Eleanor, who hated the tropics, and therefore would never journey there, despite the joy she took in being with her granddaughter—not to mention the glee Eleanor now took from interfering in Bettina's life.

"I'm perfectly comfortable, thank you very much," Bettina muttered. It wasn't Little Dix Bay, but she had no complaints. The mid-October sky was cobalt blue, and cloudless. The slightest of breezes kept the heat of the autumn sun at just the right temperature.

And the fifteen-foot wall that surrounded Eleanor's estate assured her that no reporters or photographers could accost her. With sightings of Art Cross being reported all over the Bay Area, Bettina's comings and goings were now hot scoops with the San Francisco paparazzi.

And she had no doubt that Daniel Warwick had a team of U.S. Marshals watching the house, in case the rumors were true, and Art did indeed reach out to her.

Yes, she had cabin fever. Sleep was her best option for her boredom. If only her mother would take the broad hint and leave her alone, life would be perfect, at least for a few hours.

Alas, no. To get her attention, Eleanor pinched her. "Damn it!" Bettina yelped.

"*Shhhh!*" Hera and Lily hissed in unison.

"Cursing—in front of your daughter?" Eleanor frowned disapprovingly.

This time, both of Bettina's eyes flew open. She'd forgotten that her daughter was sitting only a few feet away, meditating with Hera.

"In my defense, it's a Monday. She should be in school, not home for some trumped up holiday called 'Indigenous People's Day.'"

"Darling, it's Columbus Day. Even in your day, there was no school," Eleanor pointed out.

"Ah! Well, why didn't you say so?"

"*Shhhhhh!*" Hera and Lily hissed again.

To prove that they would not be deterred, Hera started chanting a mantra. At some point, she must have taught it to Lily too, because the little girl followed her lead.

Their eyes were closed, so they could not see Bettina give Hera the finger.

But of course, Eleanor saw it, and voiced her disapproval with a long drawn-out sigh.

I've got to get Lily out of here before she turns into Hera's Mini-Me, Bettina vowed to herself.

Just as disconcerting was Prince Vsevolod's adoration of Hera. Noting how he sat at attention at the older woman's feet, Bettina assuaged her anger by telling herself that the self-professed Wiccan had cast a spell on her poor pup.

Eleanor declared loudly over the chanters, "Darling, it worries me that you've practically become a hermit! Perhaps it's time you take a nice long drive."

Bettina raised her sunglasses to glare at her mother. "Have you forgotten the phalanx of reporters parked across the street?"

"You can exit via the old carriage alley," Eleanor countered. "They won't even know you're gone."

"Where would I go? All of my friends have deserted me. Besides, in the first trimester of my pregnancy, I shouldn't be exerting myself."

"Yes, you keep reminding me."

"So sorry that you find me repetitive," Bettina sniffed. "Hera seems to keep you aptly entertained. If I bore you, just say the word, and I'll move out."

As the women scrutinized each other in stony silence, Bettina thought: Good, she's feeling duly chastised.

This assumption melted away when Eleanor murmured, "The only thing stopping me is that there are enough homeless on the streets of San Francisco. I'd hate for my granddaughter to join their ranks."

Bettina was too angry to retort. Instead, she lowered her sunglasses and flipped over onto her back.

"Buck up, Bettina—if not for yourself, then for your children."

Bettina flinched at the weariness in Eleanor's voice, but it did nothing to take her off the defensive. "What is that supposed to mean, anyway?"

"It means that it's time to get on with your life—with or without that felon of a husband, your expensive condominium, your treasured possessions—and anything—or anyone else—you may be mourning."

Ouch.

Bettina was suddenly on guard. Was Eleanor suspicious that the child she was carrying may not be Art's after all? And, if so, how would this affect how her mother felt about her—or for that matter, her new grandchild?

She couldn't bear the thought that Eleanor might favor Lorna's newborns over hers. Only this morning, Hera let it slip that Lorna was having twins: a boy, and a girl.

She's always trying to one-up me, Bettina thought. "Just what exactly do you think I should be doing?" she snapped crossly at Eleanor.

"Oh, I don't know!" Eleanor, exasperated, threw up her hands. "If you're looking for busy work here in the house, why not decorate the nursery?"

"You mean, the room that was formerly occupied by Grandmother Connaught's washerwoman?" Bettina sniffed.

"Setting up camp in the servants' quarters was your choice, Bettina, not mine. And, you said it yourself—you won't be here forever."

"True that," Bettina nodded grudgingly. "Well then, I guess I should start interviewing stylists."

"If you say so." Eleanor's tone indicated she thought otherwise.

"If you're worried about the cost, I assure you, I'll pay you back somehow. And, of course, I'll hold to what ever budget you set."

Eleanor's eyes narrowed. "Don't be silly. The infant you carry is my grandchild. Ergo, I'll cover the cost of the room's renovation—and the whole basement suite, for that matter. My only concern is whether we can count on the discretion of an outsider."

Bettina's eyes grew large at the thought that photos of her child's room could end up as gossip fodder. Rumors would fly: had it been decorated with Art's ill-gotten gains? If so, Daniel's SWAT team would stampede through Eleanor's home too.

Her mother would never forgive her for that.

Bettina nodded contritely. "I see your point. Yes, then, I guess I will pull the room together myself. It shouldn't be too difficult. My God, it's only a nursery." Bettina bit her lip. "And, by the way, I will keep to a budget because I insist on paying you back as…well, as soon as I can. The Connaught Crosses are anything but freeloaders." She glared in Hera's direction.

If she thought it would rankle the other woman, she was disappointed. Hera's chant only grew louder.

Still, Eleanor's approving wink did much to raise Bettina's spirits. "Look at it this way, Bettina: if you screw it up, your baby will be too young to know it. Besides, you've already got a head start, what with that darling crib you purchased last month."

Bettina frowned. "Have you forgotten? It—along with the rest of my belongings—is under Federal lock and key."

"Maybe that very nice court-appointed trustee will allow you to buy it back," Eleanor suggested.

Bettina frowned. "Mr. Warwick isn't 'kind.' He's a bully."

Eleanor's right brow arched upward. "Really? Why, I thought he was rather solicitous—that is, under the circumstances."

"Not to mention a hunk," Hera chimed in, breaking her chant.

Bettina bristled as she watched the women exchange winks. Ignoring Hera, she declared, "Don't be ridiculous, Mother! The only reason he feels the need to treat *you* with kid gloves is because of your personal relationship with Judge Lawrence! As far he's concerned, I'm practically a…a gangster's moll." The less Eleanor knew about her attraction to Daniel—and for that matter, Daniel for her, the better. "Besides, if he knew how much that crib cost, he'd never give it back." Bettina pointed to the auction catalog on the side table. Because it's a Vetro, it may actually go for as much as what I paid for it: *forty-five hundred dollars."*

"For a crib? Such a waste of money," Hera murmured, mid-chant.

"I do nothing in half measures," Bettina shouted back at her.

"We're quite aware of that, my dear." Hera shrugged as she unwound herself from her lotus position in order to reach across to the table for something—

Oh no, Bettina thought. Not another of those wretched auction catalogs!

Hera leafed through it until she found what she was looking for: the two-page spread showcasing thumbnail photos of the paddles in Bettina's collection. "A picture paints a thousand words. Or in this case, a thousand pictures bring only one word to mind: ouch."

Lily opened one eye and looked over.

Bettina snatched the catalog out of Hera's hand before her daughter could see it. "Oh, my God! Where did you get that?"

Eleanor shrugged. "It came in by post. Apparently, a mass mailing went out to everyone in our zip code."

"Just great! Now, the whole neighborhood can come to it, and gawk at my humiliation." She slammed her hat so far down on her head that it covered her eyes.

"On the subject of cribs, there is always Goodwill. I'm sure you'll find several to choose from," Hera offered.

"And expose my poor infant to the vermin and lice that breed in the world of hand-me-downs?" Bettina shuddered at the thought. "I think not!"

"You know, Bettina, I still sit on the trustee board of Matthew's alma mater, Town School," Eleanor pointed out. "I'm sure I've seen a crib or two in its thrift shop, the Clothes Closet over on Polk. Or maybe it was in Final Encore—you know, the San Francisco Opera's thrift store, on Fillmore. Considering that you're on the board of the latter, perhaps you can arrange to run in—after hours, of course."

Bettina shook her head adamantly. She couldn't stand

the thought of the volunteer sales clerks—many whose PHM&T applications she'd vetoed—snickering behind her back.

"Why use a crib at all?" Hera mused. "Native societies nestle their children in their own beds until puberty. It's why they are so close and loving." Even as she clicked her tongue, she tousled Lily's hair in sympathy.

"Really?" Bettina bristled. "Did Lorna share *your* bed?"

Hera smiled supremely. "As a matter of fact, yes, she did. And you see how wonderfully well she turned out."

And she ran away from you the moment she could, Bettina was tempted to say. But she didn't. What was the point? Now that Hera was her mother's bestie, doing so would only add to Eleanor's annoyance with Bettina.

It seemed to Bettina that she could never win her mother over to her side.

Well, listening to Eleanor's suggestion this once would certainly be a step in the right direction. But how would she start?

As if reading her mind, Lily asked, "Mummy, how about this place?"

She was pointing to an Ikea Warehouse flyer that had fallen out of her grandmother's copy of that day's *San Francisco Chronicle*. Its cover showcased a room filled with nursery furniture—changing table, rocker, dresser, and crib, all painted high-gloss white—under the headline, "GREAT LOOKING, AT A SMART PRICE."

The price was ninety-nine dollars. The mattress would set her back another seventy dollars, and a highchair was fifty dollars.

It would do in a pinch.

"Emeryville isn't too far away," Eleanor declared.

"Where is that?' Lily wondered out loud.

Bettina's tone was ominous: "Across the bridge."

It was all she could do to keep from gagging from the bile climbing up through her throat. She'd been able to avoid San Francisco metropolitan area's East Bay region for more than a decade—in fact, since Matthew's graduation day from that haven for hippie heathens, the University of California, in Berkeley.

The one memory she held from that day was the acrid smell of pot that permeated the air.

Supposedly, Berkeley had gentrified in the meantime. It was inevitable, what with the stratospheric rise in Bay Area real estate costs. And with the university's international reputation, Berkeley was certainly the crowning glory of what Bettina thought of as the wrong side of the bay.

Lily clapped her hands in glee. "The bridge? Goody! It's *soooo* pretty! And I love love *love* all the big tall redwoods in Marin! Can we stop in Mill Valley for lunch —perhaps at Piazza D'Angelo?"

Bettina winced. Ah, if only the Ikea was over the *Golden Gate* Bridge, in Marin County, but no. The mammoth discount furniture outlet was certainly too downscale a store for that enclave of posh hamlets. "Unfortunately not *that* bridge, Dear. We'll be driving over the *Bay* Bridge."

"The *other* bridge?" Lily wrinkled her nose disdainfully. "But you once told Uncle Matthew that you'd get a nosebleed if you ever had to cross it to the other side." Her eyes opened wide. "Will I get a nosebleed too?"

Hearing her, Hera burst into laughter.

Miffed, Bettina shrugged, "At least there is one good thing about that side of the bay: Chez Panisse is there. You remember it, don't you Lily? Daddy and Mummy took you there for your fourth birthday!"

"Really?" Hera's jaw dropped open. "At one-hundred dollars a person? Times, three—wow! That would have fed at least thirty people at the Glide Memorial Food Bank."

That harridan! If I stay here a moment longer, I'll simply go mad, Bettina thought.

She stood up and gathered her things. Realizing she still held the auction catalog in her hand, Bettina flung it as far as she could into the pool.

The catalog floated lazily on the water for a few moments before sinking to the bottom.

"Mummy, what was that?" Lily demanded.

"The past, darling!" Bettina forced herself to smile. "The future swims ahead of us. Time for a road trip!" She held out her hands to her daughter.

Happy for anything to break up her boredom, Lily grabbed them and leapt up.

Prince Vsevolod ran after them, but Bettina wasn't having it. "Traitorous mongrel!" she hissed at the hapless creature. "You've chosen your bed. Now, lie in it!"

It was an apt metaphor, considering Hera's penchant for sleeping outside in order to, as she put it, "commune with this great city's flora and fauna."

By flora, she must have meant marijuana, because sometimes Bettina smelled it on her. As for fauna, Bettina had little doubt that Hera had fleas.

If so, it would serve Prince Vsevolod right.

1: 22 pm

"I'll look for the crib over here!" Lily shouted, as she sprinted through Ikea's cavernous showroom and out of sight.

"Wait! Don't run so fast!" Bettina hated yelling, but it was hard to catch up in four-inch Louboutins. She was dizzy, and longed to sit down—just not on one of the store's many hard foam couches.

As far as Bettina was concerned, the store's map was absolutely useless. They'd been walking around for almost two hours, nudged forward by the herd of other holiday shoppers. Equally disconcerting was that each of the store's four floors was divided into smaller quasi-rooms.

To find her way around, Bettina followed others, who in turn all followed arrows stamped onto the showroom floor, like rats given a clue in a maze.

Frustrated, she snagged one of the few showroom clerks and commanded, "I'm looking for the *Sundvik*."

The clerk frowned and blinked twice. "I beg your pardon?"

Bettina let loose with an exasperated sigh. "You work here, so you must speak Swedish!" She pointed at the crib on the catalog page. "The SUNDVIK! See? S-U-N-D-V-I-K."

The clerk snickered. "Do I look Swedish to you?" She had dark curly hair and brown eyes.

Bettina shrugged. "Admittedly, no. So now, in English, tell me: where are the damn cribs?"

The woman pointed directly behind Bettina.

"Oh…well then—"

"You're welcome," the woman muttered, as she walked away.

The crib was somewhat of a disappointment: made of wood, plain white, just straight lines with no real sense of style.

And there was only one: the floor sample.

"Wait!" Bettina tapped the woman on the shoulder. "Despite having more wear and tear than it should, I'll buy it."

"Whooptie-doodle." The sales clerk snapped her gum in Bettina's face.

Bettina snapped her fingers in the woman's face. "Well, don't just stand there! Ring it up. Or call someone else, who may actually want to earn a commission."

The clerk crossed her arms. "We don't work on commission. We work for a buck over minimum wage."

"And it shows," Bettina muttered. "I'm sure you're quite capable of writing it up anyway."

"Nothing gets 'written up' here."

Bettina presumed she was referring to rude sales clerks too.

The clerk continued, "You take this downstairs"—she pulled an item ID slip from a small clear pouch tacked on the wall, beside the crib—"to the warehouse desk. One of the clerks will pull a new one from the storage area for you, all nicely boxed, so that you can take it to the check-out queue."

"You mean, I'll have to stand in line?"

"Um…*yeah.*"

Bettina glowered at her. "I presume I can arrange for delivery at checkout as well?"

The woman's eyes opened wide as she noticed Bettina's handbag. "Are you slumming or something?"

Bettina clutched tightly to her bag. "What do you mean by that?" she asked defensively.

The woman smiled knowingly. "No, seriously, how did you come here? By limo?"

"That's a very silly question," Bettina retorted. At least, in this time of her life. "I drove myself."

"Well then, if you don't have anyone to help you put it in your car, you should grab a cart, so that you can wheel it out to your car by yourself too."

"Such nonsense," she muttered to herself. But, of course, someone would help her. After all, she was a Connaught.

And, unfortunately, also a Cross.

The one saving grace, she presumed, was that certainly none of the clerks in Ikea had lost their life savings with Art.

She snatched the ticket out of the clerk's hand, and then turned in the direction where Lily ran. The sooner they got out of there, the better.

"Mummy, what is a Swedish meatball?" Lily's question was innocent enough.

It was on the tip of Bettina's tongue to tell Lily that it was a blowzy albino whore with a penchant for breast enhancement procedures and odious soon-to-be ex-husbands, but then she noticed that Lily was pointing to a poster for the meatballs and other delicacies from the retailer's in-store café.

Rants and tirades were beneath anyone born a Connaught. Better she keep her answer simple and apropos to the question. Albeit, not *too* apropos. By now, Lily was as tired and hungry as Bettina, and thus her sudden interest in anything resembling food.

With her credit cards frozen, Bettina had just enough cash on her to purchase the crib and the mattress. She'd have to stave off her daughter's hunger until they could hit an ATM machine.

It was time for a little subterfuge. She clicked her tongue and faked a shudder. "Swedish meatballs are cow entrails rolled in bread crumbs, and covered in brown cornstarch gruel."

Lily wrinkled her nose. "Ewww, yuck!" Still, the little girl stared longingly at the feast being enjoyed by the families who occupied the tables in front of her.

They're popping those meatballs into their mouths as if they're Teucher champagne truffles, Bettina thought.

The memory of the Swiss chocolatier's best-celebrated candies made her even hungrier. She had to get out of there as soon as possible, before they both passed out.

That's when she noticed them: two women, sitting at the food bar, cradling toddlers in their arms. To their credit, they weren't chowing down on Swedish meatballs, but partaking instead in large bowls filled with what looked like herring and sour cream.

Not to their credit was the fact that they were openly staring at Bettina as they whispered to each other.

Bettina froze. She knew she was glaring, but she didn't care. She was tired and ravenous. Most of all, she was ashamed to be seen in such a downscale emporium by someone who actually knew who she was.

By tomorrow it would be all over town: Bettina Connaught Cross shopped at Ikea. She'd be the laughing stock of the Junior League, not to mention the San Francisco Opera Guild, and the San Francisco Ballet Auxiliary.

She had to get out of there—now.

Just then, one of the women took Bettina's picture with her iPhone.

Why, the audacity of that bitch!

Bettina stormed up to her. "Delete it—*now*," she growled.

The woman shook her head. "My, my, how the mighty have fallen!" She clicked her tongue in mock shock.

"If you're going to quote the Bible, you shouldn't do so while acting so cruel to others," Bettina admonished her.

"You're calling *me* cruel?" The woman snorted. "Ha! You're the one who won't let others into her club if they don't fit into a size two! I should know. I was one of your rejects."

"You have no one to blame but yourself," Bettina retorted. "Just look at all the crap you cram into your mouth. No wonder you're plump—and not in a pleasant way, either!" To make her point, she lifted a container filled with sour cream that the women must have ordered as a side dish and faked a shudder. In truth, she was so hungry, she could have lapped it up.

"I'll admit, I like to eat. Can you admit that you like being a bitch?"

Bettina abhorred losing control of her emotions. But the one thing she hated more than anything was losing control, *period*—

Which was why she snatched the woman's cell phone out of her hand, and dropped it into the container of sour cream.

The cream splattered all over the table. However, one drop flew directly into the eye of the woman's toddler.

The little boy shrieked.

"How dare you! My iPhone—it's ruined!" The woman cried out. "And you injured my son!"

"Mummy!" Bettina looked up to find Lily staring at her, mortified.

A tsunami of shame washed over Bettina. "I'm—I'm so sorry. I didn't mean for your little boy to get caught in the crossfire." She held out a napkin to the woman.

The woman yanked it out of her hand.

Not even a thank you? *How rude!*

Not to be outdone, Bettina retorted, "Do you see how your actions can backfire and hurt the ones you love? My husband's chicanery hurt my daughter—not to mention my reputation."

"Your husband wasn't the one who started a snooty-hooty mommy group. *You* did," the woman's friend pointed out. "Despite what he did, if people don't feel sorry for you, Bettina Connaught Cross, you have no one to blame but yourself."

Of course, the woman was right. There was nothing more Bettina could say—or do, for that matter.

She wanted to cry.

But not in front of these two bitches.

And certainly not in front of Lily.

She straightened her back, took Lily's hand, and walked away. But they could still hear the woman, shouting after her: "We're going to the auction. I may buy one of your size zero designer dresses as a souvenir."

Bettina's head whipped around. "Why bother? With those hips, you'll never fit into it."

The woman waved her off. "Are you kidding? I'm going to use it as a rag."

Before Bettina could reply, Lily pulled her beyond the café and down the hall.

As they passed a trash can, Bettina tossed the crib ID ticket into it.

Lily's eyes opened wide. "We aren't buying it after all?"

"No." Bettina shook her head. "Our baby deserves better."

And so do we, she thought to herself.

She kept her head down until they reached the car. Her eyes were so glazed with tears that she didn't realize she took the wrong exit out of Emeryville: not south on

Interstate 80 toward the Bay Bridge, but north, toward Berkeley.

Damn! Damn! Damn!

She glanced over at her little girl, who hadn't said a word since they left Ikea. Lily was staring out the car door window. Had she passed out from hunger?

No, but still, Bettina didn't like what she saw. Lily's lips were puckered into a scowl. A lazy tear meandered down her cheek.

She reached over and patted her daughter's hand. "I've got a great idea! Why don't we stop in Berkeley for a bite to eat?"

Lily shrugged.

"Honey, I know you're starving. I promise, we'll be there in no time at all."

Lily turned toward Bettina. With a trembling voice, she asked, "If we weren't going to get the crib, why did we cross the bridge in the first place?"

Bettina rolled her eyes. "To get out of the house, I guess."

Lily nodded at the obvious truth. "I feel as if we let the baby down," Lily's lip was quivering again. "Maybe Hera is right and it should just sleep with you."

"Never," Bettina vowed. Seeing Lily's shocked look, she added, "I might roll over and squash the poor thing in my sleep."

"You couldn't. Even that mean woman admitted that you're only a size zero." Lily took a moment to scrutinize her mother. "Mummy, was she telling the truth? Are the Feds selling everything we own? Even my American Doll collection?" Her eyes opened wide. "Even my collection of tutus?"

"No! Certainly not anything that belongs to you—just a few of my things. And…your father's."

Bettina's adamant declaration calmed her child. But, truth be told, everything left in the penthouse's closets had already been warehoused and itemized for the auction.

One way or another, Bettina vowed, I'm buying back Lily's things.

Lily's smile was wan, but it was still a smile. "Don't worry, Mummy. Since we don't have money, I'll share all my things with the baby. I promise." She turned around so that she could look behind them, to the buildings fronting the eastern side of the bay. "Maybe tomorrow we can do another road trip to Ikea, to get the crib."

Hearing that, Bettina almost drove off the road. She shrugged. "Next time we come here, we'll wear masks," she muttered.

The little girl furrowed her brow. "But what if they think we're robbing the store?"

Bettina laughed raucously. "Trust me, nobody would risk going to prison for robbing a bunch of knockoffs."

Lily laughed at that. "Even Daddy was smart enough to rob only really wealthy people, just like Robin Hood."

Bettina thought, Robin Hood? *Hardly.*

Still, the last thing she wanted to do or say was anything that might upset her now smiling daughter.

Bettina wondered what Lily would think when she learned her mother sold out her father to Daniel Warwick.

She prayed that day would never come.

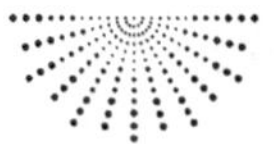

CHAPTER FOURTEEN

**Also Monday, 13 October
(a.k.a., Indigenous People Day)
1:55 p.m.**

A PICNIC, JADE REASONED. IT'S THE PERFECT ROMANTIC break for a warm, sunny day.

At least, that's what Jade told herself as she pulled her car into a curbside parking space on the Berkeley campus, several blocks from her destination: Wheeler Hall, where the English Department was located.

Over the past few weeks, Reggie's schedule was such that he was spending much more time at the university than at home. He left by seven in the morning, and on most nights he wasn't home until after ten, reasoning that he could cut the commute, and because he wanted to be available to students who scheduled appointments to discuss their term papers and theses. On the off chance he'd still be hungry, she waited on her own dinner so that they might eat together and discuss their days. But, usually, by then he'd already eaten, and was so tired that he fell straight into bed.

As he snored gently at her side, Jade asked herself, why would he want to come home to my lousy cooking and boring talk about toddlers when he's around smart, vibrant people all day long?

She'd mentioned her concerns to Jillian and Ally while stacking chairs after the Top Moms meeting.

Her fears were met with disbelief. "Okay, yeah, so Reggie spends his days talking to other eggheads about Iambic pentameter," Ally conceded. "Still, it was you who pulled him up off a sidewalk. It was you who saved his soul."

"Yes, I know! But…but…" Jade's eyes filled with tears. "People grow. And sometimes they grow apart." Stoically, she shrugged. "You know what they say: 'if you can't be with the one you love, love the one you're with.'"

"Stop it!" Jillian demanded. "Don't you get it? *You're the one he loves.* He's with you because of it."

"Then why does he find it so easy to be away from me?" Jade countered.

Ally shook her head adamantly. "You don't know if that's the case. My guess is that he misses you as much as you miss him."

"If he's there, you can be too," Jillian insisted. "You

know, like, 'if Mohammed can't come to the mountain, why not bring the mountain to him?'"

Jade scowled. "I don't get it. Now, you're comparing me to a mountain? I don't think I've gained that much weight—"

Ally laughed. "Silly, what she said has nothing to do with your weight. It has to do with reminding him why he loves you in the first place. Even professors have a lunch hour or a dinner break. Meet him in Berkeley for some face time," she winked knowingly—"or whatever. Don't forget that other grand old saying: 'absence makes the heart grow fonder.'"

To that end, Jade timed her trip over the bridge today to coincide with Reggie's lunch break.

Her picnic basket held his favorite foods: cold cider, cold roast beef sandwiches, homemade potato salad, and one of Jillian's apple-rhubarb pies. She brought a blanket that could be spread on the ground. Online, a campus map showed several parks, including one just a few blocks away called Faculty Grove. She hoped he'd take her up on her suggestion that they eat there, if only to gauge if he was proud to be seen with her. She knew there had already been a few faculty-and-spouse parties.

He never suggests we attend, she thought sadly. I guess he's ashamed of me. Today, if we run into one his colleagues, I'll make sure he sees that I can hold my own.

Just for the occasion, she purchased a short gauzy skirt, which she paired with a loose bateau-neck sweater, and little ballet pumps. Her hair fell loosely to her shoulders. Taking a deep breath, she set off in the direction of Wheeler Hall with the picnic blanket tucked under the arm carrying the picnic basket.

On three different occasions, students stopped her in order to ask directions to some other building. Shyly, she informed them that she "wasn't enrolled."

This only made her feel all the more stupid for not being one of them.

She turned the corner a few blocks beyond Wheeler Hall when she saw him. She stifled the urge to call out to Reggie when she realized he had his arm around the shoulder of some girl: a student, obviously.

So, that's Sam Hartness, Jade thought.

The woman was only a year or two younger than Jade. Worse yet, she was stunningly beautiful: slim and tall, with long dark hair, almost to her waist. Her face was graced with dimples, and large, limpid eyes. Sam wore low-slung jeans over low-heeled booties. Her plaid flannel shirt was not tucked in, and it was unbuttoned, revealing a tight white T-shirt underneath.

She and Reggie were laughing about something, and interrupting each other playfully as they debated the topic at hand. When they reached the corner and turned in her direction, Jade ducked behind a truck.

They walked right past her, turning onto Sather Road, and through the university gate, toward town.

Reggie had his hand on the small of the woman's back.

Where the hell are they going? Jade wondered. To the girl's dorm, I'll bet—for a quickie.

This is why he never comes home to me.

She couldn't help herself; she had to follow them.

When she got outside the gate, she passed a panhandler. From what she could tell, he was older than her by at least a decade. His hair, matted and filthy, grazed his hunched shoulders. His face was sallow, and he had a bad cough. Still, he lifted his head in order to mutter, "Lady, got any change?"

Jade shook her head no. Instead, she handed him the blanket and the picnic basket.

"Jesus, lady—thanks!" His fingers fumbled with the wicker catch on the basket. She knew she shouldn't stare, so she walked away quickly.

She wondered how Reggie felt these days whenever he passed someone who was homeless.

I'll bet he didn't even notice this guy, she thought. Maybe he did, but he didn't want to acknowledge him. Certainly not in front of his new girlfriend.

At that moment, Jade realized she was a part of Reggie's past.

Was she also a part of his future?

Only he could answer that question.

She set out to get her answer.

"Why don't we split a pizza?" Bettina suggested to Lily.

Lily tilted her head sideways. "Why, Mummy? You don't like pizza. You call it kid's food, and you always say it's filled with cheap calories."

It's also *cheap*, Bettina thought. But of course she'd never say that to Lily. "We're on holiday, remember? We can pretend we're in some region where pizza is a delicacy—Italy, for example."

Lily shrugged. "Okay. But must we order it with a lot of vegetables?"

Bettina shook her head. "We'll get a plain one." Since it was also the cheapest one on the menu, it made sense to Bettina. In order to hold onto the money for the crib, she could only spend twenty dollars, tops, which was all that the ATM machine spit out anyway, considering the dearth of cash in her bank account. As it turns out, a plain pizza was eighteen dollars, which left only two dollars for a tip. The waitress would not be pleased, and she was surly enough as it was.

The restaurant, called Gather, was next to the university's campus. The only reason Bettina chose it was because it seemed to be filled with students and university staff, as opposed to the typical bohemians the town was known for.

They'd just ordered their pizza when Lily declared, "What is Professor Pudberry doing here?"

Bettina followed the little girl's stare.

Lily was right: C.R. Pudberry was taking a booth on the other side of the room, with a statuesque brunette.

His advanced placement class with PHM&T's Foursies group had been a big hit, both with students and moms. He'd chosen Lily as the lead role in the class's production of *Romeo and Juliet*. The child did a stellar job. Her iambic pentameter was spot on, despite her lisp. The raves from the other mommies were the highlight of Bettina's summer.

Alas, after the final curtain call, Professor Pudberry tendered his resignation. It would have been reasonable for him and Bettina to part ways amicably. Unfortunately, Bettina's response was to shout, *"Excellent, well! You're a fishmonger!"* It was harsh, granted, but his defection could not have happened at a worse time, since she'd just learned of Art's chicanery. Locking in Pudberry for another year of A.P. classes would have gone far to halt the exodus that was to follow.

The professor's response was cool indeed. "Madam, you're quoting from *Hamlet*. Had your education been more complete, it would have dawned on you that a more fitting sendoff would have been from the play you've just seen—say, something along the lines of, *'The hate I bear thee can afford no better term than this: thou are a villain,'* or say, *'A plague on both your—"*

"This should suffice," she interrupted him, and then honored him with a middle finger salute before walking off.

Despite the passage of two months, her anger hadn't quelled. Noting the telltale signs of her mother's fury— the narrowing of her eyes into laser-sharp slits, and the flat-lining of her attempts to keep a stiff upper-lip smile— Lily stroked her mother's cheek. "Mummy, Professor Pudberry was very nice to me."

Bettina took the hint. She nodded and opened her mouth to put the child's mind at ease, when out of the corner of her eye, she saw someone else they knew:

Jade.

Had Bettina doubted the rumors that Jade and Pudberry were an item, the Pierce woman's appearance, here and now, certainly put it to rest.

She watched as Jade's eyes scanned the room, finally lighting on the professor.

Bettina almost laughed out loud at Jade's tearful stare.

Talk about a comeuppance for the brainless little tart, she thought.

Now, to make things a bit more interesting…

WHEN JADE FINALLY SPOTTED REGGIE, HER HEART FELT AS IF it leapt into her chest.

She wondered, What do I do now? Should I confront him? Should I accuse him of…of…

Of what? Taking a lunch break with his assistant?

And how would she answer his question of why she was here in Berkeley, let alone in this exact restaurant?

Run—right now. Before he sees you. Before you say something foolish.

Before he realizes he's stuck with a loser.

But before she turned around, she heard too loudly and certainly imperiously: *"Jade! Jade Pierce! Yoo-hoo, darling! Over here!"*

Jade had heard the voice so often that it was unmistakable to her: Bettina.

Everyone looked up and around—including Reggie.

Jade stood there, frozen in her mortification. But then, she felt someone tugging on her hand.

It was Lily. "We ordered a pizza. Would you like to eat with us?"

Jade nodded numbly.

Lily held her hand as she guided her to Bettina's table.

Jade forced herself to look straight ahead, to avoid her instinct to look back at Reggie, to see if he saw her too.

But of course he had. Bettina made sure of that.

By the time they reached the table, she hadn't decided whether to slap Bettina silly for calling her out, or to kiss her for saving her from shame.

She chose the middle ground: an air kiss.

She'd make sure to pick up the check. She owed Bettina that much.

∿

SMALL TALK. IT WAS THE ONLY THING THEY HAD IN COMMON.

At least, Jade hoped so. Unfortunately, every attempt on her part hit a brick wall.

For example, Jade asked Bettina if she liked the restaurant.

Bettina rolled her eyes. "It's my first time here. I'm not expecting Chez Panisse."

Jade tried again: "How has your pregnancy been this time around?"

Her polite question was met with a frosty one-word utterance: "Fine."

At a last attempt at civility, she asked, "Isn't it exciting that Lorna is having twins?"

Bettina ignored the question. Instead, she asked, "Who is that beautiful woman with professor Pudberry?"

So, Bettina has seen him too.

Jade shrugged. "His student assistant."

"What a stunning young lady!" Bettina's declaration was enthusiastic, even in jest. "And a Berkley graduate student at that! With those legs, she could trod the boards on a fashion runway! Go figure!"

Jade shut up until the pizza arrived at the table.

They were chewing in silence when suddenly Lily exclaimed, "Mummy, Professor Pudberry is coming this way!" The way Lily's eyes lit up, you'd think they were going to be honored by the presence of a rock star.

Jade glanced down at her plate.

Reggie's kiss on her cheek was such a surprise that she

almost bumped heads with him. By the time she looked over, he'd slipped into the booth beside her. "Fancy meeting you here." He then smiled at Lily. "And with my favorite Juliet of all time."

Lily blushed. When she stared up at him again, her sweet little voice rang out true and clear:

"'Take him and cut him out in little stars
And he will make the face of heaven so fine
That all the world will be in love with night
And pay no worship to the garish sun.'"

The restaurant went quiet before its patrons burst out in applause.

Lily stood on the bench and bowed.

Jade glanced over in time to see the pride on Bettina's face. Feeling Jade's eyes upon her, she looked away shamefully.

She didn't call me over as an attempt at friendship, Jade realized. She saw Reggie first, and wanted to embarrass me. Well, she certainly succeeded. I hope she's happy about it.

Suddenly, Jade realized that Reggie's lunch partner hadn't followed him over. She frowned at him. "Why am I here? No reason, I guess—just having lunch somewhere different, so why not this side of the bridge?"

Her defensive tone surprised Reggie enough to take the smile off his face. "Why didn't you call? I would have waited lunch for you, had I known." His reply took in Bettina and Lily as well.

"You seemed in good hands." Bettina craned her neck. "Where is your gorgeous little companion? She had no need to run off because of us."

"Our lunch break isn't long, and someone has to man the office. Sam will cover for me until I get back," Reggie said evenly.

"She must love working under such a renowned scholar," Bettina simpered. "And I'm sure she loves the honor of being at your beck and call."

Reggie's glance shifted between Jade's petulant frown and Bettina's knowing smirk. The lay of the land was now obvious, even to him.

He frowned as he looked down at his watch. "I should head back as well. I'll see you at home, Jade. Great running into you, Lily." He honored Bettina with a slight bow. "Wish I could say the same for you, Lady Macbeth."

As he walked away, Lily asked, "What did he mean by that, Mummy?"

"It's his way of being clever," Bettina muttered. She turned to Jade. "It seems to me you deliberately gave him the impression that we came here together, for some sort of ladies' lunch. Ha! As if." She nodded toward the other tables, which were mostly filled with students. "Is there trouble in Paradise? Come on Jade, you know you can count on me."

"*Count on you?*" Jade was livid. "All you've ever done is use me, or make fun of me, or be cruel to me." She stood up. "And now you mock me and my relationship with Reggie? You're as bad as Kimberley!"

At the utterance of her nemesis' name, Bettina sat up straight. "Kimberley? What does that witch have to do with anything?"

"Other than doing her best to make my life miserable? Nothing!" Jade retorted. "Speaking of Kimberley, a word of warning, Bettina—" The bemused sneer on Bettina's face stopped her cold. "On second thought, never mind. Whatever she has planned for you is well deserved."

Jade threw down a twenty and a ten before stalking off.

"What? ...Wait!" Beckoning Lily to follow, Bettina grabbed her bag and ran after her.

It was all Lily could do to keep up with them.

JADE PRACTICALLY RAN DOWN THE BLOCK.

"Jade, please—wait!" Bettina cursed the fact that her high heels made it almost impossible to catch up. There were just too many people on the street. Shoppers and students dodged the panhandlers begging for change, and the petitioners trying to buttonhole them to sign their clipboards.

One such do-gooder cornered Jade as she waited for the crossing light to change. Jade shook her head, but the petitioner—bearded, his hair pulled into a man-bun—wouldn't take no for an answer.

At least it allowed Bettina to catch up with her. "Jade, I demand to know what you meant by that remark about Kimberley!"

"Excuse me!" Man-Bun butted between them. "We were in the middle of a conversation. As I was saying, just a few dollars will help us stop the poaching, before the crocs go into extin—"

"Stand in line." Bettina shoved him out of the way. "You can't just walk away like that, Jade," she pleaded.

"Oh, yeah?" Jade countered. "Watch me."

Bettina took hold of her arm. "No—please. You see, you're right! She has it out for me, and—"

Man-Bun grasped Bettina's arm.

As Bettina wrenched it away. Instinctively, she smacked Man-Bun away with her handbag.

Man-Bun grabbed it from her hand. Staring down at it, he cried, "Her bag—it's crocodile!"

Bettina glared back. "Of course it is! And it's Hermés, so I suggest you remove your soiled claws from it, post haste!"

By now, a crowd had gathered. Three of the others also had clipboards. The backs of the boards were stamped: PETA. As leverage, two of the petitioners grabbed hold of their compatriot.

Because she was sorry to see her outnumbered, Jade held Bettina tightly around her waist.

A ninety-five thousand-dollar handbag should hold up under the circumstances, but it had never been tested for a melee of this sort. When the handles ripped apart, the tag holding the lock flew off in one direction, the clochette holding its keys in another.

When the bag hit the ground, and Bettina's belongings spilled out across the sidewalk.

One of the panhandlers grabbed for her things. Just as Bettina lifted her foot to stomp on his hand with her heel, Lily yelled, "Mummy, please don't hurt the sad old man!"

Bettina froze.

Not Jade. She scooped up Bettina's bag and her keys, and hustled Lily across the street with her.

Bettina stumbled after them.

They reached Bettina's car first. Bettina's hands were shaking so hard that she dropped her keys twice before she finally hit the remote lock.

Lily hugged Jade before climbing into the passenger seat.

"I guess I should thank you for saving us," Bettina muttered.

Jade shrugged. "I'd prefer a little respect. But if that's impossible, I understand. What I don't understand is why you're always so cruel, Bettina."

She walked away before Bettina could answer her.

"The nerve of her!" Bettina declared.

"Is she right?" Lily asked. "Do you like being cruel?"

"No! Of course I don't..." Bettina's voice trailed off as

a cold shiver ran down her spine. *Oh, my God! Does Lily think that I'm* cruel?

Maybe not now. But someday she'll realize it.

And she'll hate me.

The thought kept her silent all the way home.

REGGIE CAME HOME A LITTLE PAST EIGHT.

He found Jade on their bungalow's flat roof, where she could watch the headlights of the traffic crawl over the Golden Gate Bridge, just beyond the dome of the Palace of Fine Arts.

She didn't turn around when he sat beside her on the other wicker chair facing the bridge, or when he lifted her hand to his lips in order to kiss her palm.

Finally, he broke her silence by asking, "So, what was that all about?"

She sighed. "I thought we'd have a picnic."

"You and Bettina and Lily?"

"No!" It angered her that he couldn't see the obvious. "I came to Berkeley for you."

He shook his head, incredulously. "Then how did you end up with Bettina inside the Gathering?"

Jade took a deep breath. "Sheer coincidence. I walked in there because I followed you and…and *Sam.*"

He peered closely at her, but the shadows made it difficult for him to read her eyes.

"I saw you walk out of Wheeler Hall," she added. "You seemed to be enjoying her company—a lot. Anyone could see that."

"I like her sense of humor," he admitted. "But that's all."

"Really? That's all?" It was hard to keep the quiver out of her voice.

"She's a gorgeous girl. But then, so are you, Jade."

"But she's more than just gorgeous. She's smart, too."

"And so are you." He held her hand to his face. "So why don't you do something about it?"

"Do something…like what?"

"Take classes in something you love. Brady shares custody, and will be willing to work out the childcare aspect. Financially, you have the breathing room. You've got the time. So, what do you say about it?"

"Would you like me better if I was smart?"

"You're one of the smartest, most vibrant women I know. You're not yet twenty-five, and already you've lived a fuller life than some women twice your age." He pulled her into his lap. "I love you now, Jade Pierce, with all my heart, and that will never change. But it's time you love yourself."

Indignant, she muttered, "What makes you think I don't?'

"If you did, you wouldn't be insecure when some ninny like Bettina tweaks your nose about your past—or your future, for that matter. Be honest with yourself: the only one holding you back is you."

"You're right. I know it." She shivered—not just because of the night chill, but because the thought excited her.

"What kind of courses would you take?" he asked.

"In high school, I loved history," she admitted. "Especially anything to do with art."

He nodded "Berkeley has an art history major. It's a small department, but it's got one of the largest digital resource libraries in the world, and it's tied to both museums on campus."

"Sounds interesting." Her heart pounded in her chest at the thought of doing something so exciting.

"But, first things first," he cautioned her. "The easiest way to get into Berkeley is to first register for the next semester at San Francisco City College, where you can finish the first two years of your undergraduate degree. Besides being closer and more convenient, it allows you to take one course each semester at Berkeley. The better your grades, the more likely Berkeley will accept you as a full transfer." He snapped his fingers. "In fact, I've got a pal in the Art History Department. He's looking for help with archiving the digital photos from his many trips to other museums around the world. If you were to offer to help—"

"Yes! Of course I will. Reggie, this is—*perfect*!" She was so excited that she kissed him hard, on the lips.

He kissed back—just as hard. When their lips parted, he whispered, "No more jealousies?"

"No more jealousies. I don't want to live my life like Hamlet." She chuckled shamefully. Then, fervently: *"Doubt truth to be a liar / But never doubt I love."*

Reggie's smile glowed with admiration. "You know, if you wanted to change your major to English Lit—"

She silenced him with a quick peck. "The last thing I need is for the other students accusing me of being teacher's pet. 'Friendly but not familiar'."

Reggie frowned "Who said that?"

"Woody Allen. *Broadway Danny Rose.*"

He stood up with her in his arms. "You never cease to amaze me."

"'You ain't seen nothin' yet'."

She proved it all night long.

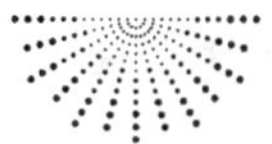

Halloween
Wednesday, 31 October
6:37 a.m.

"YOUR CLEOPATRA COSTUME IS ADORABLE!" JILLIAN ASSURED Mary, Life of Pie's shop manager.

Surprised, Mary looked up as she placed one of the special order mini-pie boxes on the kitchen worktable. "It's a bit tighter than I'd like, but then again, I work at the best pie shop in the world." She looked Jillian over as well. "So, I take it the big day is finally here—pitching pies at the money men?"

"I guess so." Jillian rolled her eyes. "Each day melts into the next. I'm so tired that I can't see straight. Thank goodness the PHM&T members voted down homemade costumes! I didn't have to make the twins' costumes for the Halloween contest today, like last year."

She turned full circle in a new white silk suit, which she'd paired with a hot pink silk shell that peeked out from above the jacket's first button. "What do you think? It's from Nordy Rack. Do I pass inspection?"

"I'll say. Especially in those killer heels!" Mary gave a low whistle.

"I borrowed them from Jade." Jillian winced. "They're a little tight, but the color was right. I didn't have time to chase down a pair before this meeting, what with how busy the shop has been these past few days."

"You're telling me! We've done so many pumpkin pies, it's unbelievable! And we can't make the pumpkin pie-lets with the jack-o-lantern faces fast enough. Oh, and at the very last minute, we got a special order from Kink." Mary rolled her eyes. "They wanted pecan log 'penises' and pumpkin pie-let va-jay-jays from our new 'Edible Unmentionables' line, for special attendees to their 'Orgasmic Haunted Halloweenie' event."

"Note to self," Jillian muttered, "Leave Brady out of any brainstorming sessions for special order products. Speaking of which, where have you stashed the pie-let samples for the meeting?"

"Top shelf, on the right...no, the left." She was still staring at Jillian's shoes. She shook her head in wonder. "Right...I hope you're not walking all the way to Silicon Valley in those heels."

"Nope. Brady ordered a limo for us, so that we arrive in style. Ally and he are picking me up here, along with the pie-let samples." She sighed. "As it is, we'll just barely make it back in time for the Chestnut Street Tot Parade at one o'clock."

Just then, the rattle of the locked front door caught their attention.

"I'd better open. The natives are getting restless," Mary declared. She ducked back into the shop, but a moment later she was back. "Jillian, better shake a leg! Your limo just pulled up to the curb."

"Wave at them so that they know I'm on my way!" Considering the height of the top shelf, for once this morning Jillian was happy that she was in the heels.

They clacked on the wood floor as she hurried out the door with the boxes of pies.

9:47 a.m.

"IS THERE ANYTHING WE NEED TO KNOW ABOUT THESE GUYS? You know, for small talk purposes?" Jillian's question came after three recitations of her short and sweet speech on her love of pies, and her process for 'lovingly testing each flavor' before launching them in public.

Brady thought for a moment. "To be honest, I doubt there will be much time for chitchat. The venture capitalists stack up these appointments like planes coming in for landing at SFO. Just wait for my cue, smile, and launch in."

Ally nodded. "With a caveat. I know that Owen Acworth can be somewhat talkative—at least, he was with me."

"That's because he was crushing on you—" Brady interrupted.

Ally silenced him with a nudge in his side. "That may be the case, but if so, try to bring up the fact that you like to jog because he does too." She wrinkled her brow in thought. "As for Teddy Collins, he's more of the tech nerd who hit it rich, and mostly sits there and nods. On the other hand, Liam Markham is the numbers cruncher. He's strongly conservative"—she wagged a finger at Brady —"so no off-color jokes."

"Got it," Brady and Jillian said together.

"I'm starved," Brady announced. "Let's share one of the mini-pies, three ways." He reached for the box.

Ally slapped his hand away. "No way! With our luck, Jillian will get crumbs all over her nice new suit, or the pie you choose will be Teddy's favorite flavor, or something."

At that moment. The limo slowed to a crawl.

Ally looked out the window. "Besides, we're already here. You can wait until we're in the conference room, and coffee has been served." She pulled out a compact in order to dab her lips with a color wand. "Smile, people! It's show time!"

She was the first out of the limo when the driver opened the door. "Brady, grab the pie boxes, okay?"

"Yes ma'am," he grumbled, as he turned to Jillian and muttered, "Is she this bossy on the playground too?"

"Nah," she assured him. "Only you bring out this side of her." She patted his cheek. "Not to worry! I had Mary pack two pecan pie-lets, because I know it's your favorite."

"Maybe I fell in love with the wrong Top Mom," he teased. "After you, partner."

THEY WERE KEPT WAITING FIFTEEN MINUTES BEFORE A MAN— mid-forties, in an expensive blazer over a white T-shirt and designer jeans, but sockless in John Lobb loafers— opened the conference room door in order to shuttle out two guys, both wearing hipster glasses and slouchy jeans with T-shirts touting the latest Comic-Con.

Jillian felt overdressed.

He glanced over her before shaking Brady's hand, and grabbing Ally in a bear hug.

I guess he's Owen Acworth, Jillian thought.

"Ally, darling, aren't you a sight for sore eyes!" The way his eyes roamed over her, anyone would think he meant it quite literally. "So sorry to hear this guy here"— he stuck a thumb toward Brady—"swept you off your feet before I had my chance." He then turned to Jillian. Proffering a hand, he added, "But if Ms. Frederick's pies live up to their hype, at least I can admire your balance sheet." With the other hand, he motioned toward the conference room. "Shall we?"

THE CHILL EMANATING OFF OWEN'S PARTNERS WAS ENOUGH to send a shiver up Jillian's spine.

Teddy Jenkins was wary and silent, whereas Liam Markham barely looked up when they walked in. When he finally did so, his eyes bore into each of them, one after another.

His handshake was limp at best.

An assistant placed the pie boxes in the center of the expansive white granite conference room table, beside the silver coffee service. When Brady suggested that he cut the string on the boxes, Owen waved him away. Instead, Owen simply asked, "Jillian, why pie?"

She took a deep breath and started talking.

Later, she'd wonder why she went off script. It was as if all the things she memorized went out of her head. Instead, she talked about making her first pie—apple—at the age of four, with her grandmother. And how her grandmother explained that, in order for her to really claim the pie as her own, she had to do all the work herself: set the temperature on the oven and roll out the dough. Then she sliced the fruit, and measured out the spices—all to her grandmother's exact instructions.

The exotic smell of baking pie meant happiness, she explained. Its first bite was sheer joy. The pleasure started at the tongue, before coursing through the body, then stopping at the heart. "With pie, we make memories. More to the point, we share the memory, and our love."

When all three men nodded, she knew she had their attention. She glanced over at Ally and winked.

Ally clicked onto her laptop computer. Life of Pie's marketing strategy appeared in the monitor on the wall beside them. "Gentlemen, let me lead you through our success to date…"

It's perfect, Jillian thought. We can do no wrong.

All three men nodded through Ally's portion of the pitch, enthralled at the raves from customers—through pictures and comments posted on various social media, and via the handwritten love notes that were pinned on the store's large pegboard wall. Their products' broad demographics won them nods, as did their product mix, and the success of new product launches, including the mini-pies, and special event marketing for weddings and corporate parties.

When Brady took over and relayed the cold hard financial facts—Life of Pie's rapid growth, the national trends for the growing demand for pie, and the need to be the first retail chain out of the gate—all three men were scribbling furiously on the pads in front of them.

Finally, Owen laughed. "Cut it out, dude! All this potential is making my mouth water."

Brady smiled. "Good, because I'm famished. Shall we dig in?"

The partners of Collins, Acworth, and Markham exchanged smiles and nods. "Sure, why not?" Liam Markham waved toward the boxes.

Brady motioned to Jillian. He snapped the string on the boxes, but held out the knife to her. "I'll let you do the honors, partner."

Beaming proudly, she opened the box—

To see six gigantic pecan log penises inside.

There were also six pumpkin pies, each glazed to resemble a woman's most intimate part.

Brady didn't know why she froze. No matter. Every performance had its climax.

He too looked into the box: Yep, those were quite some climaxes.

Instinctively, the others rose and looked too.

Liam Markham scowled. Without a word, he walked out of the room.

Owen gave a long, low whistle. "Well, Brady old boy, I must say, this is a first." He shrugged. "Glad I had a big breakfast. What say I walk you folks to the door?"

1:10 p.m.

ALLY FELT IT WAS TO BRADY'S CREDIT THAT HE KEPT SILENT until they were out of the limousine and back in her townhouse before exploding at Jillian.

"What the hell were you thinking?" he shouted. "What part of 'conservative' did you not get?"

"I…Okay, yes, it's my fault! Mary said they were on the top shelf, on the right…or the left…Oh, I don't know anymore! I guess I picked up the wrong boxes by mistake!" Her sobs made it impossible to clearly make out her words.

"You mean, you didn't pack the box yourself? You didn't open it to make sure it didn't contain a six-pack of penises?" Brady swung around to Ally. "You were right. We should have left her at home."

Jillian turned to Ally. "Is that what you said—that I shouldn't have been there with you?"

"No, of course not!" She glared at Brady. "My exact words were that Brady shouldn't force you into doing anything that made you feel uncomfortable—including making presentations, since not all of us worship at the Tao of Steve Jobs." She stood up so that she and he were nose to nose. "And, by the way, if I remember correctly, Life of Pie's Edible Unmentionables was your idea."

He was about to retort when Ally's cell phone buzzed.

She frowned. "It's Owen. Ha! This ought to be good." She clicked on the cell. "Hi, Owen…Ha, ha, yes, we sure pulled one over on you guys, didn't we? Listen, we are all *so* sorry…um…What did you say?" Her eyes opened wide. "Yes, sure, of course we're open to another powwow…but no, no pie this time? …Okay, I'll have Brady and Jillian put it on their calendars. Good-bye."

"Wow. Just…wow." Brady threw his hands up in the air. "What did he say?"

"Just that they sent a couple of their assistants into the shop to get a bunch of pies to bring back to the office. Not only have they sampled our pies all week, but a few from other specialty bakeries in the Bay Area as well. Hands down, the consensus is that our pies are the winner."

"But…he says he wants to meet without more pie." Jillian wiped away a tear.

Ally snickered. "Only because it's affecting his waistline. So, no more pie until his trainer whips him back into shape. In the meantime, they're ready to talk real figures."

"Maybe I shouldn't go," Jillian murmured.

Ally squeezed her hand. "He specifically asked for you. So, yes, you'll be there."

"I don't know. Let me think about it." She picked up her purse and headed for the door.

"Jillian, wait!" Brady ran after her. When he caught up, he blocked the door with his arm. "I was way out of line to talk to you in that manner. Please, forgive me."

She tossed his arm aside. "Be honest, would you be saying this if Owen hadn't called back?"

"In all honesty, *yes*. We've all made a rookie mistake or two. We accept it, we learn from it, and we move on."

"Rookie mistake…yeah." Jillian shrugged. "Listen, Brady, I love what I do—"

He nodded. "And it shows."

"Let me finish." She took a breath. "As I was saying, I love it so much that the moment it quits being fun, I'll figure out something else to do to feed my family. So, here's my proposition: if my learning curve is going to get you so upset, feel free to back out as our financial guru. Now, if you'll excuse me, I want to join my twins before the parade starts."

She headed out the door.

He shook his head in wonder. "What did I say wrong?" he asked Ally.

"Oh, I'd say just about everything." She put her arm around his waist. "Hey, look on the bright side. There's a big commission in this for you, and it further burnishes your reputation as a Silicon Valley rainmaker. Now, if I can just keep you from making Jillian cry, we just might have a success on our hands." She squeezed him tightly. "You're the love of my life, but she's my business partner. When it comes to Life of Pie, making her happy is what comes first, always."

"Okay! Fine!" He kissed her. "From now on, I listen to the referee—that is, you."

"And don't you forget it." She reached for her purse. "Come on, we've got to save Jade from Zoe burn-out.

Barry and Christian each got Zoe a princess costume, after I specifically told them I'd already bought one for her. Zoe threw a fit because she wants to wear all three, so I left them with Jade. I hope she was able to talk the little hellion into wearing just one."

Brady sighed. "Boys are so much easier. Any super hero with a cape will do."

"You won't be saying that in another fifteen years. Just you wait and see."

He knew she was right, as always.

1:22 p.m.

THE CHESTNUT STREET HALLOWEEN PARADE, WHICH BEGAN at the Moscone Recreation Center, must have started a few minutes before Jillian got there. Now that PHM&T's membership was twice as big, columns of mothers were already meandering down the street with their little fairies, princesses, pirates, hobgoblins, witches, and super heroes in tow. As always, the youngest club members were first in line, carried in their mothers' arms, if not snuggled in a sling or riding high in a baby carriage.

The moms were also in costume, invariably naughtier ones than those of their charges. A French maid holding an angel in her arms was apt to make heads turn, as was a slinky feline in a catsuit holding a dog-eared fuzzy puppy toddler.

Jillian left on her business suit, figuring it to be shocking enough for her friends to see her in.

Even stopping at each of the street's shops for candy, the Twosies mommies and their toddlers were already as far down as Avila Street, in front of Books Inc.

"Oh, my God—Jillian!" Jade, dressed as a ballerina, held up her hand and waved frantically at her friend. She wasn't smiling, just relieved. "You're finally here!"

Jade stood with Lorna and the rest of the Twosies moms. Amelia and Addison—dressed as Tweedledee and Tweedledum—were being pushed in their stroller as Jade held Oliver—in an Iron-Man outfit—on her hip. Dante, dressed as one of many Ant-Mans, was being pushed in another double stroller, along with Zoe, now dressed in a pink princess gown.

Noting Jade's concerned look, Jillian exclaimed, "I'm so, so sorry! It ran a little longer than we anticipated—"

"Wait…no one told you?" Lorna grabbed her by the hand. "I know I left at least six messages on your cell!"

"I haven't looked. I turned it off during the meeting." Jillian rushed to the stroller to look at her daughters. "Is something wrong with the girls?"

"No, not at all! It's just that…" Lorna paused, as if collecting her thoughts into words. Finally, she whispered, "Scott and Victoria…they're dead!"

"What?" Jillian took a step back. Her heart was

pounding so rapidly in her chest that she felt faint. "How…"

Lorna steadied her friend. "The call came in from San Francisco General. Apparently, he had you down as his next of kin. They were in their car. It was parked at a red light when another car plowed through the intersection and hit them, head on. Little Scotty—"

"Scott's baby!" Tears filled Jillian's eyes. "Is he—"

"No, not at all! By some miracle, the child doesn't have a scratch on him," Lorna assured her. "But, Jillian…" Lorna and Jade exchanged worried glances. "The hospital is expecting you to…to claim the bodies, and to take Scotty."

"*Me*?" Jillian shook her head, as if that could wake her from this nightmare.

She felt a hand on her shoulder: Matt's. The next thing she knew, he sat beside her. He gave her a bear hug.

"I asked Matt to bring the car around. I'll take you to the hospital," Lorna explained.

"I'm going too." Ally's voice came from behind them. At some point, Brady and she must have walked up just as Lorna was relaying the awful news, because they looked as shocked as she felt.

Brady kissed Jade's cheek as he took Oliver in his arms. After taking hold of the twins' stroller, he kissed Ally too. "Call us when you get to Jillian's house. Matt and I will meet you there with the children. By then, Caleb should be home too."

Matt stood. After kissing Lorna goodbye, he took hold of Dante's stroller, and heaved Zoe onto his shoulders.

The little girl squealed with delight.

With Ally holding one arm and Jade holding the other, Jillian stumbled onto her feet.

As they walked silently to the car, all she could think about was Scott's last words to her:

I may not have shown it at the time, but I want you to know that I'll always cherish our years together, Jillian. I wish you my best.

Don't worry, Scott, she vowed silently. Your children will always know of you.

"NOT TO RAIN ON OUR WONDERFUL LITTLE PARADE, BETTINA, but have you noticed that the rest of the Twosies Top Moms have deserted you—*and* their children?" Kelly's question was delivered with a snicker, which she followed with a wink to Kimberley.

Like Bettina, they were dressed as witches, which annoyed Bettina to no end, especially since it was obvious that their costumes were much more costly than her bargain basement cape and pointed hat. Bettina's big splurge was for the tutu Lily had seen and begged for in the 1887 Dance Shop's window, on Union Street.

Bettina's head whipped around just in time to see Lorna, Ally, Jade, and Jillian round the corner.

She looked for her nephew's stroller, and was relieved to see Matthew pushing it. He was walking their way, with Brady Pierce.

Lily ran up to them and gave her cousin a kiss on the cheek. Matt tousled her hair fondly.

When they reached Bettina, she growled, "Where the hell are your wife and her friends going?"

"And Happy Halloween to you too," Matt replied. "Hey, aren't you moms supposed to be in costume?"

Lily giggled.

Before the women could retort, Brady warned, "There's been a death in Jillian's family—the twins' father, Scott. Jillian's friends know she needs them now, so do them all a favor and give them a break, if just for today."

The women gasped in shock, but kept their mouths shut.

At least until Brady and Matt moved on.

"What a bastard," Kimberley muttered.

"What do those guys see in those women, anyway?" Kelly huffed.

"It's because they're nice to everyone," Lily replied.

"Well, out of the mouths of babes," Kimberley murmured.

Kelly frowned down at Lily. "No one asked you."

Bettina resisted the urge to slap Kelly across the mouth. Instead, she took her daughter's hand, and walked off.

What did I do to deserve those bitches in my life? she wondered.

But, of course, she already knew the answer to that.

2:47 p.m.

"Yes, she is Victoria Dunne." Jillian stared down at the photo of the broken, lifeless face of the woman who had stolen her husband. Finally, she turned her head in the hope that the morgue technician would take the hint and put it back in its file.

Her friends were not allowed in his office with her. In hindsight, Jillian knew it was for the best. She didn't need them hearing her when she gasped and sobbed over the next picture:

Scott.

His face was swollen and badly bruised, his scalp was caked in blood, and half his teeth were missing. His eyes were closed, as if he were sleeping.

Don't worry, Scott. I'll look after ours.

Ours. But, what about his?

Right now, Scotty lay in Ally's arms, suckling a bottle.

I'll have to call Scott's parents, and Victoria's too for that matter.

She sighed at the enormity of the task ahead of her.

She handed the photo back to the morgue tech. "Scott Frederick."

Rest in peace, Scott.

3:34 p.m.

ALLY WAS ALWAYS THE FIRST TO ADMIT SHE WAS A LOUSY cook. Today was no exception. However, she added the caveat, "Hey, Jade is no better."

"At least I have Little Star Pizza on speed dial," Jade pointed out.

By the time Jillian and her friends reached her house, Brady had already retrieved their order, and had opened a couple of bottles of wine to boot.

While the others ate along with the children, Jillian locked herself in her bedroom and dialed Scott's attorney.

He was shocked with the news of Scott's passing. "Jillian, I know you have a lot of arrangements to make, but do come in at your earliest convenience. As the executor of his will, you'll have to—"

"What do you mean?" Jillian sat down hard on the bed. "He must have changed his will!"

"No. I have it here in front of me. He had arranged for me to meet with him and Victoria after their wedding. She had no will at all, so any update on his would have happened then too. My understanding is that your divorce wasn't going to be final until early November. In the state of California, the will stays in effect if a spouse dies prior to the divorce decree. So, as it stands now, you are still the will's executor, and in it he also calls you out as the sole guardian of his children."

"But—but what about the child he had with Victoria?"

"Victoria has no siblings. Both her parents are in their seventies and her father suffers from Parkinson's disease. I presume her mother has her hands full with his care. Let me give you their telephone number, in Vermont. The fact that Scotty has half-sisters close to his age may be comforting for them to know…"

Her hand shook as she rang off the phone.

She braced herself for the shock and tears that would meet her next two calls: to Victoria's parents, and Scott's mother.

I think I'm going to faint, she thought.

At that moment, she realized she hadn't eaten all day.

She went downstairs instead.

"THEY'RE ALL ASLEEP? IT'S A MIRACLE," JILLIAN MURMURED.

"The parade wore them out," Jade reasoned.

Caleb sat in the rocker. Scotty was cradled in his arms. The infant's eyes were closed, and his lips quivered while he dreamed.

Jillian walked over to him and knelt down to kiss Caleb.

When their lips parted, his eyes went back to the infant. "He's so tiny. He resembles the girls, doesn't he?"

Jillian nodded. "Yes. The shape of his nose, I guess. And he's just as blonde. I think his eyes are Victoria's, though." Her voice trailed off.

"I want a son, someday," he assured her. "Our son."

Our son.

How will I tell him that I already have a son to raise?

She was relieved that Matt, Lorna, Brady, Ally, and Jade now surrounded them. Ally handed her a glass of wine, and one to Caleb as well.

Everyone raised their glasses.

Jillian's toast was simple: "To the happiness of all our children."

—To Be Continued—

NEXT UP!

TOTLANDIA: Book 6 (The Twosies/Winter)

Winter's chill isn't just in the air. It also runs through the veins of all the women in the Pacific Heights Moms & Tots Club. Besides dealing with the politics of the Pacific Heights Moms & Tots Club, Lorna discovers a secret that will scandalize the members—and perhaps have one one them leaving in disgrace; As for Jade, her new part-time job on the UC Berkeley campus allows Reggie to see her in a whole new light—one that will either make, or break, their relationship; Jillian is juggling too much—not just the twins, the growth of Life of Pie, and the details of her wedding, but the guardianship of the infant, Scotty. Will her fiancé, Caleb man up to fatherhood—or will he be scared off by threats of a lawsuit from Rona, the mother her deceased ex-husband, Scott? And Brady's frustration over Ally's refusal to commit to marrying him leads him down a slippery slope–into her past. And finally, Bettina's idea for a new mobile may get her out of hock—but will it keep her in the good graces of Daniel Warwick— the Federal agent chasing down, Art?

OTHER BOOKS BY JOSIE BROWN

The True Hollywood Lies Series

Hollywood Hunk

Hollywood Whore

The Housewife Assassin's Series

The Housewife Assassin's Handbook (Book 1)

The Housewife Assassin's Guide to Gracious Killing (Book 2)

The Housewife Assassin's Killer Christmas Tips (Book 3)

The Housewife Assassin's Relationship Survival Guide (Book 4)

The Housewife Assassin's Vacation to Die For (Book 5)

The Housewife Assassin's Recipes for Disaster (Book 6)

The Housewife Assassin's Hollywood Scream Play (Book 7)

The Housewife Assassin's Killer App (Book 8)

The Housewife Assassin's Hostage Hosting Tips (Book 9)

The Housewife Assassin's Garden of Deadly Delights (Book 10)

The Housewife Assassin's Tips for Weddings, Weapons, and Warfare (Book 11)

The Housewife Assassin's Husband Hunting Hints (Book 12)

The Housewife Assassin's Ghost Protocol (Book 13)

The Housewife Assassin's Terrorist TV Guide (Book 14)

The Housewife Assassin's Deadly Dossier (Book 15: Series Prequel)

The Housewife Assassin's Greatest Hits (Book 16)

The Housewife Assassin's Fourth Estate Sale (Book 17)

The Housewife Assassin's Horrorscope (Book 18)

More Josie Brown Novels

The Candidate

Secret Lives of Husbands and Wives

The Baby Planner